"I'm not inhuman, McClintoch."

"Ah." He nodded and touched his forefinger to the center of her lower lip. "That's nice to know."

"And—and I don't much relish the possibility of being left here alone."

"I see." The tip of his finger traced the seam of her mouth. "In other words, given the choice between tolerating my intolerable presence and tolerating only your own, you'd sooner cast your vote for me."

"Yes. No. McClintoch, don't do that!"

"Don't do what?" His finger stroked across her lip again. "This, you mean?"

SANDRA MARTON is an American author who used to tell stories to her dolls when she was a little girl. Today, readers around the world fall in love with her sexy, dynamic heroes and outspoken, independent heroines. Her books have topped bestseller lists and won many awards. Sandra loves dressing up for a night out with her husband as much as she loves putting on her hiking boots for a walk in a southwestern desert or a northeastern forest. You can write to her at P.O. Box 295, Storrs, Connecticut 06268 (please enclose a SASE).

Books by Sandra Marton

Sandra Marton

EMERALD FIRE

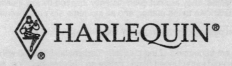

TORONTO • NEW YORK • LONDON
AMSTERDAM • PARIS • SYDNEY • HAMBURG
STOCKHOLM • ATHENS • TOKYO • MILAN • MADRID
PRAGUE • WARSAW • BUDAPEST • AUCKLAND

ISBN 0-373-12100-8

EMERALD FIRE

First North American Publication 2000.

CHAPTER ONE

SLADE MCCLINTOCH was at the reception desk of the Hotel Florinda when he first saw the woman. She was coming down the rickety wooden steps that led into what passed for a lobby, the expression in her blue eyes as cool as the white cotton dress she wore, and the sight of her was so incongruous that Slade almost forgot how annoyed he was with the rat-faced little man lounging behind the desk.

She paused on the last step, her hand on the banister. Tall, slender, her face a pale oval beneath a short, shining cap of golden hair, she was about as perfect a sight as a man could hope to see in New York or San Francisco, let alone in this God-forsaken town on the edge of the Peruvian jungle—and disapproval was etched into every line of her beautiful face.

Well, why wouldn't it be? Slade thought, with a lift of one dark eyebrow. The only thing attractive about the Hotel Florinda was its name. Nobody, not even the most dedicated optimist, could find anything to like in the cheap furnishings, smeared walls and worn floorboards.

Its singular claim to fame was that it was the only hotel in Italpa. That was why Slade was here. As for the woman—why *she* was here was anybody's guess. From the looks of her, she was probably a tourist who'd strayed from her group. There were increasing numbers of them down here lately, pampered rich folks happy to shell out whatever it cost to taste the dangers of the savage jungle—but at a safe and sanitized distance.

Whatever the woman was, she was as out of place in this grim setting as an Amazon orchid would have been in a tangle of sawgrass.

'A lovely flower, is she not, *señor?*'

The desk clerk leaned toward Slade over the scarred mahogany counter, a sly grin on his rabbity face. For a second, Slade wondered if he'd spoken his thoughts aloud. No. He was tired—but not tired enough to have begun talking to himself. Not yet, anyway, although if he didn't get some sleep soon...

The clerk bent closer. 'She is a sight to behold, yes?'

Adrenaline surged through Slade's veins. He worked in a world of men; he knew such speculative comments about women were commonplace, knew, as well, that, as such remarks went, the clerk's was mild and harmless. Still, he didn't like it. Maybe it was the man's shifty smile or the way he lowered one eyelid in an exaggerated wink.

Or maybe, Slade thought, forcing a smile to his lips, maybe it was just that he hadn't had any sleep in damned near fourteen hours.

'Indeed,' he said pleasantly. 'She is almost as lovely as this charming establishment—for which, I assure you, I have a reservation.'

The clerk pursed his lips. 'I will check again, *señor,* but—' His shoulders rose then fell in a gesture of eloquent distress. 'I still do not see your name on my list.'

Slade fought to keep the smile on his face. He had been patient, even gracious; he had played the game, which involved pretending innocence even as he slipped the sleazy little man a fistful of *intis*, and now, by God, he'd had enough.

Perhaps the clerk wanted a bigger bribe. Perhaps the reservation was truly lost. Perhaps a miracle had occurred and the Florinda had turned into a tourist mecca, booking suites and deluxe accommodations to high society. Hell, anything was possible here, on the edge of the Amazon.

Slade didn't give a damn. He was exhausted. He was short-tempered. He wanted a cold beer, a hot shower and a soft bed. He wanted the room he was entitled to, and he wanted it now.

He counted silently to one hundred while the clerk made an elaborate show of thumbing through a stack of papers.

'It is as I feared, *señor,*' the little man said finally. 'There is no reservation in your name. I cannot imagine what we can do to solve this problem.' His hand crept to the desktop where it lay palm up, fingers lightly curled, like a rhinoceros beetle that had been flipped on its back and awaited salvation. 'Unless you can, perhaps, think of some solution…?'

Slade smiled, his teeth flashing whitely against his tanned skin. He crooked his finger, motioning the clerk closer, and the man obliged, smiling slyly in anticipation of more *intis*.

'I can, indeed, think of something,' Slade said, very softly. His eyes, as cold as green glass, locked on the other man's and he whispered a few words in Spanish.

The clerk's smile turned sickly. He reached under the counter and came up with a key dangling from a brass tag.

'*Ay, caramba,*' he said in amazement. 'Look at this,

señor. I have found your reservation. Such a foolish error. You will forgive it, yes?'

Slade grinned. 'Certainly.' He reached across the scarred desktop, patted the clerk lightly on the cheek, and picked up the key. 'We all make errors from time to time.'

'You are most gracious, *señor*. May you have a pleasant stay at our humble establishment.'

Slade nodded as he turned away. A pleasant stay? Only if you believed in miracles, he thought as he strode across the lobby. The best he could hope for was that the roaches weren't bigger than rats, that the sheets would have been changed this month, that...

Damn! What room was he in, anyway? He hadn't asked, and he should have. The Florinda was four stories high, and that fourth floor would be the only one that was bearable. Scowling, he dug in his pocket for the key and held it up, trying to read the number on the worn brass tag. With luck, noise from the street wouldn't carry to the top floor. There might even be a breeze from—

'Oof!'

The collision was swift and forceful. There was a whisper of silken hair across his chin, the faint drift of jasmine in his nostrils. He reached out and clasped a pair of slender, feminine shoulders.

'Sorry,' he said, 'I didn't mean to—'

He stopped in mid-sentence. It was the woman he'd noticed a little while ago. Close up, she was more than beautiful. She was stunning.

'I didn't mean to run you down,' he said, smiling as much in appraisal as in apology, 'but—'

'That's quite all right.' Her tone was frigid, and if

moments before her face had registered disapproval, now it radiated disgust.

Slade's smile thinned, but hell, he could hardly blame her. He knew how he must look—the emergency call that had brought him here had taken him straight from a work site and the hours of travel that had followed would have done nothing to improve his appearance except to rumple his jeans further and add another layer of dust to his boots.

'If you'll excuse me,' she said pointedly.

He looked at his hands, still wrapped lightly around her shoulders.

'Oh. Oh, sure.' He let go of her and smiled again. 'Sorry. I—'

'You're wasting your time.'

Slade blinked. 'I beg your pardon?'

'I said, you're wasting your time. And mine. I am not interested in a tour of Italpa.'

'I didn't—'

'Nor am I interested in seeing the jungle by moonlight.'

'Well, I'm glad to—'

'And I certainly have no wish to buy a genuine shrunken head or a stuffed alligator or anything else you might want to sell me.'

Slade's eyes narrowed. 'That's a relief. I unloaded my last shrunken head yesterday.'

A snort of muffled laughter drifted toward him. He turned sharply and glared at the desk clerk, who flushed and looked away, but not in time to conceal the smirk that curled over his mouth.

A dull wash of color rose along Slade's high cheekbones as he swung back to the woman.

'Listen, lady—'

He was talking to the air. Her shoulder bumped him as she brushed past. He stood still for a moment, and then he turned, marched after her, and caught her by the arm.

'The first thing to learn about going slumming,' he growled as he swung her around, 'is that you ought to be prepared for what you're likely to find.'

Color flew into Brionny Stuart's face. She stared at the man, at this creature who smelled of sweat and dust. She'd seen his performance with the poor desk clerk, how he'd taken satisfaction in bullying a man half his size, and then he'd turned his attentions to her. Had her really expected her to greet him with a smile?

She gave him a slow, contemptuous look, one that went from his scuffed boots to the shadowy stubble on his face.

'I couldn't agree more,' she said coldly, and before he had time to react she turned on her heel and strode away. She could feel the man's eyes boring into her back and she had to fight the almost overwhelming desire to hurry her pace.

Stupid, she thought. What she'd just done was stupid! You didn't taunt a man like him in a place like the Florinda, but after a week in this miserable river town her patience was worn thin.

Professor Ingram had warned her about Italpa, about the bugs and the filth, the heat and the unsavory opportunists who hung around its mean streets, but he needn't have bothered. This might have been Brionny's first expedition as a graduate student but it was hardly her first time in the field. Her father, a prominent archaeologist himself, had taken her with him on digs from childhood on.

Henry Stuart had grumbled about the sort of men who

hung around places like Italpa, too. Liars, leeches and worse, he'd called them, looking to steal fortunes in antiquities from the scientists who found them.

Unfortunately, Brionny had had to learn that truth for herself.

Her blue eyes darkened as she remembered her seventeenth summer, when a dark-eyed Latin Lothario had wooed her under a Mexican moon, gaining her trust and parlaying it into a job at her father's dig site when two of his regular workers fell ill.

The end of the story had been painfully predictable. The man had made off with a fortune in relics, her father had been furious, and Brionny had been left heartbroken, humiliated—and a whole lot wiser.

Wise enough to be immune to the kind of smooth operator who'd just come on to her, she thought now as she peered down a grimy service corridor that deadended off the lobby of the Hotel Florinda. Some women might have found him attractive, with his green eyes and his broad-shouldered, lean-hipped body, but she certainly wasn't one of them. If anything, she was turned off by his sort.

Brionny sighed. Actually, the only man who interested her right now would be short, squat and whitehaired.

'Where the devil are you, Professor?' she muttered under her breath.

The Ingram expedition was leaving in the morning on its quest for the legendary Eye of God, and there were still checks to write and last-minute things to buy. And, since Professor Ingram was not just half the team but the only half with the authority to sign checks and approve purchases, nothing could happen without him.

Brionny paused outside what passed for the hotel din-

ing room and pushed open the door. Mismatched
wooden chairs leaned drunkenly against stained tables;
rainwater dripped from a hole in the ceiling. Except for
a procession of large black ants that marched deter-
minedly up and down the far wall, the room was empty.

Damn! Where had Ingram gone? It was unlike him
to disappear. The most positive thing Brionny could say
about him, aside from his brilliance as an archaeologist,
was that he kept to his schedule. He was impossible
otherwise—autocratic, unpleasant, unforgiving—and
more than willing to load her with work in the face of
what she suspected might be a decline in his health. It
was hard to tell; Ingram did not take kindly to personal
questions.

'You are my assistant, Miss Stuart,' he'd said sharply
just yesterday, after she'd thought she'd noticed him
suddenly going pale at lunch, 'not my keeper.'

But then, she hadn't become Ingram's graduate
assistant for his charm. He was a leading expert on Amazonian Indian culture; even her father had been impressed when she'd gotten the appointment. Of course,
Henry Stuart would have preferred if it she'd entered
the graduate program at the university where he was
head of the archaeology department, but Brionny had
made it clear she wanted to succeed on her own.

Or fail, she thought with a little sigh. Where the devil
was the professor? She'd checked everywhere: in his
room, at the market, in the town square, and now in the
Florinda's public rooms—the lobby, the card lounge,
the dining room...

Ahead, in a dimly lit hallway, a small neon-lit sign
blinked on and off. 'AR,' it said, and she wondered
idly how long it had been since the 'B' had gone dark.

There seemed little chance of finding Ingram in the barroom, but she knew she had to check.

A pulse of screeching music drifted from beneath a slatted, swinging door. She reached toward it, then hesitated. She thought of the man who'd come on to her minutes before. She remembered how he'd terrorized the desk clerk, how he'd looked at her as if she were something that had been gift-wrapped just for him, how his green eyes had turned to chips of ice when she'd rebuffed his unwanted advances.

It would be hell to find a room full of men like him on the far side of the door.

It would be worse to have Professor Ingram blame her for forfeiting their appointment.

Brionny took a deep breath, set her shoulders, and pushed open the door.

Music swirled around her, wafted along on a pungent breath of cigarette smoke and liquor fumes. She coughed, blinked her eyes against the artificial darkness—and felt her heart plummet to her shoes.

The good news was that Edgar Ingram was definitely not in the room. The bad news was that the men who instantly turned toward her made the man in the lobby look like a candidate for Boy Scout of the Year.

Brionny swallowed. Her mouth opened, then closed. 'Sorry,' she said briskly. She swung around quickly—but not quickly enough. A man had already slipped from one of the stools that ran the length of the bar and started in her direction.

'*Buenas noches, señorita.*'

She looked up. He was not tall, but what he lacked in height he made up in girth. He looked like a barrel, Brionny thought, with tree trunks for arms and legs. He

grinned, flashing a smile that revealed shining gold teeth
and clouds of bad breath.

Brionny smiled politely. 'I'm afraid I don't speak
Spanish,' she said, lying without hesitation. 'If you'll
excuse me—'

'Iss no problem, *señorita*.' Barrel Man grinned and
put a beefy hand on her arm. 'I speak the Anglish perfect.'

'You certainly do,' she said brightly. 'Now if you'd
just—'

'I buy you drink, yes?'

'No. No, thank you very much, I'm not thirsty.'

Her answer brought a roar of laughter. 'She no
thirs'y,' he said to the room at large. The men who
understood him chuckled, then translated for their fellows. Within seconds, everyone was laughing gaily.
Brionny smiled too, although it wasn't easy.

'Would you let go of my arm, please?' she said politely.

Barrel Man chuckled. 'Why?'

'Why?' Brionny swallowed drily. 'What do you
mean, why? Because-because—'

'We danze,' he said.

'No.'

'Yes.' His arm slid around her waist.

Brionny dug in her heels. 'No,' she repeated, her
voice sharp. 'I have no intention of—'

She gasped as his hand dropped low on her hip.

'Dammit,' she snapped, grasping his wrist, 'don't do
that!'

Barrel Man shot a sly glance toward his friends.
'Dammit,' he mimicked in a high, mincing voice, 'doan
do that!'

'You have no right—'

His hand curved around her bottom. Oh God, Brionny thought—and all at once a dangerously lazy voice spoke from behind her.

'She's right, pal.'

Brionny and Barrel Man both swung around. The man from the lobby stood silhouetted in the doorway, his posture relaxed yet definitely threatening, shoulders back, arms flexed, legs slightly apart. He looked, she thought, as if he was ready to take on the world.

'Let go of the lady,' he said softly.

Barrel Man smiled. 'Why should I?'

The man smiled too. 'Because she belongs to me.' Brionny's head came up sharply. 'She's my woman,' he said, flashing her a warning look. 'Do you understand, *compadre?*'

Whether Barrel Man understood or not was debatable, but Brionny suddenly did. I can get you out of here, the man in the doorway was saying, but only if you cooperate.

As choices went, it was better than nothing.

She took a breath, smiled, and tossed her head so that her hair flew back from her face.

'Well,' she said, 'it's about time. Where have you been?'

He grinned. 'You see how much she loves me, *compadre?*' His smile vanished and he looked straight at Barrel Man. 'For the last time, man. Take your hand off her.'

There was a moment that seemed to stretch on forever. Everyone in the room seemed to be waiting, waiting—and then the man standing next to Brionny laughed and, with exaggerated care, lifted his hand from her backside.

'You mus' keep a better watch on your woman,' he said.

The man in the doorway smiled. 'You're right. I looked away for a couple of seconds and, *caramba*, she was gone.' He looked at Brionny, then raised his band and crooked his finger at her, just as he had done to the hapless desk clerk. 'OK, baby,' he said. 'Let's go.'

His eyes locked on hers and she could see the warning burning like a cold flame in their green depths. Don't do anything stupid, he was saying; this isn't over yet.

She stepped away from her admirer and walked toward him, her gaze locked on his face. He still had that lazy look about him but she could see how deceptive it was. He was ready for trouble, perhaps even hoping for it.

'Don't stop now, woman!'

She looked up, not realizing her steps had faltered until she heard that low-pitched warning. Her rescuer, it you could call him that, was still smiling, but she could hear the tension in his voice, see it in the way his eyes kept scanning the room behind her.

Her legs felt like lead. She took a step, then another, and he reached out impatiently, wrapped his hand around her wrist, and tugged her forward. She fell into the hard curve of his arm, her body molding against his side.

'Hello, lover,' he said, and he bent and kissed her, hard, on the mouth. 'Smile, lady,' he growled, his lips against her ear. 'Smile as if you mean it—unless you'd rather give our friend with the mouth full of nuggets another shot at getting lucky this evening!'

Brionny forced a smile to her face. 'You're despicable,' she whispered.

He grinned. 'She says I'm irresistible,' he called to the watching men, then added something in Spanish that made them roar with laughter as he led her out the door.

As soon as they were in the corridor, Brionny shoved her elbow into his ribs.

'You can let go of me now,' she said.

'You're welcome,' he answered, hustling her down the hallway at his side.

'All right. Thank you for your help. Now let me go.'

'When I'm good and ready.'

'Dammit, are you deaf?' She was trotting along on her toes, struggling as much to match his stride as to free herself from his unwanted embrace. 'I said—'

'I know what you said.' His arm tightened around her as he marched her toward the lobby. 'It's what *I* say that counts right now.'

'Listen here, mister, you may have saved me from— from an embarrassing situation, but that doesn't give you the right to—'

'Embarrassing?' He stopped dead and swung her around to face him, his eyes glaring into hers. 'Is that what you call that little scene I stumbled into? Hell, if that's all it was, I'll take you straight back to the boys and—'

'No!' Brionny spoke quickly, almost breathlessly. 'I—I wouldn't want to go back there.'

He nodded. 'I'm glad to see you've got some kind of brain in that head.'

She flushed. 'All right. I suppose I do owe you a thank-you, but that doesn't mean—'

'What in hell were you doing in there, anyway?'

'Look, I don't owe you—'

'You just got done telling me you did.'

She glared at him. 'I said I owed you my thanks, not an explanation, Mr-Mr—'

'McClintoch. Slade McClintoch. And I still want to know what you were doing in the bar. Come to think of it, what in hell are you doing in the Florinda?'

'I'm a guest here, if it's any of your business.'

'The Florinda doesn't have ''guests'', it has poor unfortunates who have no choice but to spend the night under its roof.'

Brionny smiled coldly. 'I couldn't have said it better myself.'

'Come on, baby, tell the truth. You're with one of those fancy tours and you went off on your own to see how the other half lives.'

'Damn you!' Brionny twisted away from him, dug furiously into her pocket, and pulled out her room key. 'Is this good enough to convince you that I belong here?'

He looked at the key, then at her. 'Either your travel agent's crazy or you are.'

'Thank you for that wonderful piece of information. Now, if you'll excuse me—'

'The next time you're desperate for a drink, go down to the corner, buy a fifth of tequila, and take it to your room.'

'Yes. I'm sure that works wonderfully for you, Mr McClintoch. But I happen to have been looking for someone—not that it's any of your business.'

Slade grinned. 'Yeah? Well, you sure as hell found someone, didn't you?'

'How dare you speak to me that way?'

'You're lucky I'm speaking to you at all. I could have taken one look at the mess you'd stirred up—'

'Me? I didn't stir anything up. Those men—'

Footsteps sounded in the hall. Slade looked up. The guy who resembled a barrel with legs was ambling toward them, flanked by a couple of his buddies. When he spotted them, his pace quickened.

Slade glanced at the woman, standing there with her room key dangling from her fingertips and fire blazing in her eyes.

'Shut up,' he hissed.

'I won't! Just who do you think you—?'

He cursed, snatched the key from her hand, and swung her up into his arms. She squealed and punched him in the shoulder as he strode into the lobby, hard enough so that he knew that beneath the curving softness of her body there was some surprisingly firm muscle.

'Put me down! Do you hear me? You put me down this minute!'

'*Señor.*' The voice and the footsteps accompanying it were closer. 'Hey, *señor,* has the lady change' her mind?'

The woman in Slade's arms was struggling harder now. And she was still mouthing off, calling him every kind of bastard, demanding he set her on her feet. If she didn't start behaving herself, he thought grimly, they were both going to be in trouble.

'Dammit, lady,' he growled as he made his way past the goggle-eyed desk clerk and started up the stairs. 'I told you to keep quiet.'

'I won't!'

'You will,' he said, and covered her mouth with his.

It was not a real kiss, it was simply a way to convince anybody who needed convincing of his ownership, to silence the damned fool woman until he dumped her in her room. It was the only way he could think of to get the both of them out of there without first having to take on The Barrel and Company, although Slade was beginning to think that might not be a bad idea, considering his growing irritation at how quickly a rotten day was getting steadily worse.

What the kiss wasn't supposed to be, he thought as he jammed her key into her door and elbowed his way into her room, was something that would turn him inside out. But hell, that was the way it felt. And when he kicked the door shut, dumped the woman on the bed and looked down at her, he took one look at her flushed face and glazed eyes and knew that that was the way it had felt to her, too.

'Damn,' Slade said softly, and he came down beside her on the bed and kissed her again.

CHAPTER TWO

TWO WEEKS later, standing knee-deep in a tangle of reeds beside a jungle pool, Brionny thought of Slade McClintoch—something she did with regularity but certainly not with pleasure—and muttered a word that would have put Professor Ingram's hair on end, had he been there to hear it.

But the professor was back at their campsite, sitting propped against a tree, making yet another entry about the Eye of God in his personal journal while the native cook prepared lunch.

Making journal entries was all he'd done since they'd found the Eye two days ago. The professor wasn't well; Brionny was sure of it now. And it worried her. He was seventy if he was a day, and they were a million miles from nowhere. When she'd tried questioning him, he'd given her as sharp-tongued a reply as he had in Italpa.

'My health is my concern, Miss Stuart. Keeping records is yours. This is the find of the century and I want it well documented.'

There was no arguing with his logic. The Eye would make Ingram's reputation and go a long way toward establishing her own. That she couldn't seem to work up the proper level of excitement was entirely Slade McClintoch's fault.

'The bastard!' she hissed into the silence surrounding the pool.

It was ridiculous that remembering a man she would surely never see again should spoil such an achievement. Other expeditions had tried to find the Eye but with no success. Ingram had put in years of painstaking research and half a dozen prior field trips, most of them made before Brionny had been born. It had all paid off. He'd gone straight to the ruins of the Forbidden City, then to the statue that contained the emerald.

'Ahh,' he'd sighed as he'd wrenched the stone from where it had lain for centuries. 'Be grateful you were part of his extraordinary event, Miss Stuart.'

'I am, sir,' Brionny had said. She'd reached out, touched the stone—and suddenly thought of Slade McClintoch, whose eyes had blazed with fire like the emerald's when he'd come down beside her on the bed in her hotel room.

With a choked cry, she'd pulled back her hand. Ingram's bushy brows had risen in surprise.

'Superstitious, Miss Stuart?' he'd said with a hint of contempt.

Brionny had grasped at the excuse. 'No, sir,' she'd said, somehow managing to smile, 'but you must admit it's not every day you get to risk the Curse of the Mali-Mali, is it?'

Of course, she thought as she unstrapped the webbed belt at her waist and laid it beside the pool, she hadn't really meant it. She came from a long line of scientists who scoffed at superstition. The gear that hung from her belt was a link to her distinguished heritage—light in weight but heavy in tradition. The battered water canteen had accompanied her maternal grandfather through the jungles of Asia and Africa. The brass-handled camp knife had been with her father's father on his explorations in Central America. And the pearl-handled revolver had been her own father's companion on his expeditions to New Guinea.

'You never know what to expect in the field, Brionny,' he'd said solemnly when he'd handed it on to her.

Or in the bedroom, she thought, and her face flamed.

Dammit! How long was she going to be plagued by the humiliating memory of what Slade McClintoch had done to her? She sank down on a fallen log and began unlacing her boots. It was like having a film clip stuck in her head. All she had to do was let her guard down and it would start to roll.

She kicked the boots off and peeled away her heavy socks, her jaw tightening as she thought back to the way McClintoch had scooped her up, marched her through the lobby. The humiliation of it. And then he'd kissed her, the typical reaction of a primitive male trying to assert dominance over an assertive female.

And then—and then...

Brionny blew out her breath. And then he'd dumped her on the bed, and everything had gone wrong.

She remembered looking up, seeing the darkness of his eyes.

He's going to kiss me again, she'd thought, very calmly.

She should have slugged him. Or raked his face with her nails. Or kneed him in the groin. She should have done *something*, dammit! Even throwing back her head and letting out a yell would have been an improvement over what she *had* done—which was nothing. Absolutely nothing. She'd lain there like the log she was sitting on and-and—

She sprang to her feet, yanked her T-shirt over her head, and tossed it on a shrub. Who was she kidding?

If only she really *had* lain there like a log! But she hadn't. What she'd done was rise to the kiss like a trout to a well- cast fly.

And McClintoch, the bastard, had taken advantage of that instant of insanity. He'd drawn her close in his arms, slipped his tongue between her lips. Sometimes she thought she could still feel the hardness of his body pressing against hers, smell his scent, taste the heat of his mouth. She could feel the brush of his fingers as he lifted her blouse and cupped her breast...

'Damn you, Slade McClintoch!'

She yanked down the zipper of her denim shorts, pulled them off, and high-kicked them on to the shrub next to the T-shirt. At least she'd come to her senses before it was too late, recognizing what he was up to, that he was taking advantage of her disorientation and turning it into fun and games time for his own selfish pleasure.

There was grim satisfaction in recalling the glazed look on his face when she'd begun to struggle beneath him. It had been the look of a man who'd almost managed to snag a prize he knew he didn't deserve and suddenly saw it being snatched out from under his nose.

'No, sweetheart,' he'd whispered huskily, his breath a sigh against her lips, 'don't stop now.'

But she had, pounding her fists against the rock-hard wall of his shoulders, telling him to get the hell off her. When he'd drawn back and stared down at her as if she'd gone crazy, she'd rolled away from him, yanked open the drawer of the rickety bedside table, pulled out her father's revolver, and jammed it into his side.

Oh, that moment was worth remembering!

'Get up,' she'd said, while the color drained from his face, and he had, by God. He'd risen obediently to his feet, then tried to sweet-talk her into putting the gun down, into admitting that she'd been a willing participant in the kiss and not the outraged victim of his insufferable ego.

And then he'd moved, fast as lightning, his hand clamping down on her wrist, his leg thrusting between hers and sending her tumbling off balance. When it was all over, the revolver was in the corner and she was sprawled across the bed—back in McClintoch's arms.

'A word of advice,' he'd said with a mocking smile. 'A woman who pulls a gun should first learn how to use it.'

'I know how to use it,' she'd started to say, but he'd kissed her into silence, his mouth moving on hers with swift arrogance, although that time his kiss had done nothing but turn her rigid with fear.

She needn't have worried. McClintoch had rolled away from her and risen to his feet.

'Relax, baby,' he'd said with a contemptuous smile. 'I'd sooner sleep with an anaconda.'

Then he'd strolled to the door, opened it, and vanished from her life like a bad dream.

A bad dream, she thought, shuddering. Yes, that was what his brief intrusion into her life had been, a bad dream. And now, she thought as she stepped into the water, now it was time to set it aside and forget it had ever happened. She would concentrate on what came next—first the long trek back to Italpa and then the exciting business of bringing the Eye home to the museum in triumph. A year from now she'd have her doctorate, and Slade McClintoch wouldn't even be a memory.

She sighed, luxuriating in the silken feel of the water. It felt cool in comparison to the hot, breathless stillness

of the air. She glanced around before reaching behind
her and unclasping her bra, but there was nothing to
worry about. Who was going to see her? The campsite
was easily half a mile away. She drew back her arm
and the bra went sailing into the reeds.

'To hell with you, Slade McClintoch,' she yelled,
took a breath, and dove beneath the water. She came
up sputtering in the centre of the pool just as a pair of
scarlet macaws swooped overhead. The birds landed on
a branch, cocked their handsome heads, and shrieked.

Brionny pushed the wet hair back from her face.
'What is it?' she said, laughing. 'Do you think I'm being too harsh on the man? Believe me, I'm not. He's a
number one, *el primo* rat. That's just what I'd tell him
if I ever saw him again.'

Which, thank heaven, she would not.

Smiling, she fell back into the water and let herself
drift. She felt better than she had in days. Maybe it was
finally getting wet all over instead of just being soaked
with her own sweat. Maybe it was saying out loud what
had been bottled up inside her for two weeks. Whatever
it was, she felt free. It was as if she'd exorcized a ghost.
Slade McClintoch was gone, poof, just like that. She
would never think of him again, never—

'I don't believe it,' a voice roared. 'Dammit, woman,
what in hell are you doing here?'

No, Brionny thought, no, no, no—

She dug her feet into the sandy bottom, shoved forward, and stared across the water.

'Oh my God,' she whispered, and dove for cover.

It couldn't be. But it was.

Slade McClintoch was standing on a rise just across
the way.

*   *   *

No, Slade thought; no, it couldn't be.

But it was. It was the woman from the Hotel Florinda, Brawna Stevens, or Brianna Smith—dammit, what was her name? He'd asked the desk clerk before he'd left the hotel—

Brionny. Brionny Stuart. Her name had slipped his mind but nothing else about her had. The cap of shining golden hair. The eyes as blue as summer and as wide as a fawn's. The way the soft curve of her breast had felt, thrusting against his hand—and now the quickest glimpse of that breast, rising rounded and full, tipped with pale rose, a flower blooming softly against the green water of the pool.

His body tightened as memories rushed back. The feel of her in his arms. The heat of her, and the perfumed scent—

The unyielding obstinacy of her. The disdain. The ease with which she'd shoved a gun into his gut.

His face set in grim lines as he made his way toward the water. The woman was a spoiled brat. He'd grown up poor in a town owned by people like her; the contempt with which she'd treated him brought back a thousand ugly memories. He knew exactly how she viewed anyone she deemed unfit to exist on her social plateau.

The only unusual thing about Brionny Stuart was that she had a damnable ability to be in the wrong place at the wrong time. She'd managed it at the Florinda and she was managing it now, in the middle of the jungle, lolling around as if she were in a backyard swimming-pool where there was nothing evil lurking in the shadows.

Slade fought back the desire to spin around and check out the jungle behind him. There was no need to do it, not after he'd already done it a dozen times in the past couple of hours, ever since a Mali-Mali arrow had gone zinging into a tree just ahead of him. After enough years in places like this you knew when something was meant to kill you and when it was meant to warn. The arrow had been a message, but he wasn't sure how to read it. Was he being told to go back, or was he being warned away from something that lay ahead? He had to know, before he could send any of his people into possible danger, and so he'd gone on, not knowing exactly what he was looking for but certainly not expecting to find this.

Ahead, in the pool, the woman finally surfaced, just enough so her head and neck stuck up from the water. What in hell was she doing here? There was nobody cleared for this area but his surveying crew and a couple of archaeologists—bad news in itself, considering what they were after. It was touchy enough bringing a crew and equipment into the jungle. Letting a pair of dried-up scientists look for and maybe walk off with a sacred stone would only make matters worse.

Dammit, but this place was getting as crowded as Central Park on a summer Sunday. A construction crew. A pair of weasely mummies from some museum. And now whatever party of tourists the woman was with—God, what a mess.

Slade put his hands on his hips, glared at Brionny Stuart, and let her have the full force of his anger.

'Get out of that water,' he snarled.

Brionny's mouth firmed. 'You can't frighten me,' she said, wishing the words would make it so. Her heart was hammering so hard she was afraid it was going to explode.

He laughed in a way that made her blood go cold. 'Want to bet?'

'I'm not alone,' she said quickly.

'I agree. Your bath tub's probably teeming with life. Piranhas. Leeches. Water-snakes.'

'It isn't,' Brionny said quickly. Too quickly. He was trying to scare her, and she was helping him do it. 'I checked,' she said, with more assurance than she felt. 'Anyway, I didn't mean that. I meant that I didn't come down here by myself.'

Slade made an elaborate show of looking around. 'No?'

'No. My guides—'

'Come on, Miss Stuart, stop the bull. There's no one here but you and me. Now, get your tail out of there. Fast.'

'I'm not alone, I tell you. If you so much as take a step closer, I'll scream.'

'You'll...' He shot her a look that was part incredulity, part disgust. 'By God, lady, you have one hell of an inflated opinion of yourself. What do you think's going on here?'

'I know what's going on,' Brionny said, mentally measuring the distance from where she crouched to the bank where her pistol lay hidden among the reeds. 'You've been following me, and—' His bark of laughter cut her short. 'What's so funny?'

'You. You're what's funny. You think I've followed you for the past—what's it been since that night? Ten days? Two weeks? Do I look like some love-smitten boy?'

'You expect me to believe it's just coincidence that's made you turn up here?'

Slade glowered darkly and folded his arms over his

chest. 'One of life's lousiest lessons is that fate is not necessarily kind. Do us both a favor, OK? Get out of that pool before I come in and get you.'

Brionny looked toward the bank again. If he'd let her get to her clothing, that would put the pistol within arm's length.

'I'm counting to three, lady. One. Two. Th—'

'Let me get my clothes,' she said, nodding toward the adorned shrub.

'Go ahead.'

'Turn your back first.'

He glared at her, his face expressionless, then shrugged. 'Two minutes,' he said impassively.

He turned away, his long legs planted firmly apart. Brionny hesitated, then paddled furiously for the bank. Water cascaded from her body as she rose and stepped on shore.

'Ninety seconds and counting.'

The bra. Where was the bra?

'Eighty seconds.'

Never mind the bra. She grabbed her T-shirt, tugged it over her head with shaking hands. Her shorts clung to her wet underpants, then snagged as she zipped them up.

'Fifty seconds. By the time I turn around, you'd better be—'

He heard the click of the safety as she released it. Son of a bitch, he thought wearily, and raised his eyes to the sky.

'Turn around, Mr McClintoch.'

'Listen,' he said, 'you're making one hell of a mistake.'

'I said, turn around.'

He did, slowly, his hands lifted. Well, he thought,

despite what had happened in the hotel room, she was right. She knew how to use the gun. She was standing erect, holding it in a no-nonsense, two-handed grip. Her hair was plastered to her head, her feet were bare, she wore no make-up at all that he could see. Except for the sweet, lush outline of her breasts beneath the damp T-shirt and the long, curved line of her hips and thighs, she looked like a fourteen-year-old—a fourteen-year-old with a gun she wasn't afraid to use.

'Take it easy,' he said quietly.

She looked at the gleaming machete that hung from his belt. 'Drop that machete, Mr McClintoch, and then start walking this way.'

'Sure.' The machete fell to the ground. 'Just do me a favor. Put the safety back on, will you?'

Brionny waved him towards the foot trail that led back to camp. 'I said, start walking.'

'Sure,' he said again, and as he did he shot a horrified look over her shoulder and yelled, 'Look out!'

Even as she spun around, Brionny knew she'd been had. But the realization came a second too late. Slade was on her instantly, moving with the speed and grace of a big cat. They fell to the ground together, rolling over and over, his hand clasping her wrist, forcing the pistol up and away.

'Let go of me, you bastard,' she panted.

'Let go of the gun,' he said.

'No! No, I—'

His hand closed over hers. The shot was an explosion of sound, echoing and re-echoing across the little clearing. The macaws screamed and rose up with a whir of wings, and then there was silence. Slade was lying across her, one hand still clasping her wrist, the other clutching the gun.

'Now you've done it,' he said softly.

Brionny's pulse began to gallop. 'Yes, I have. They'll hear that, in camp; they'll come after me—'

He rolled off her and got to his feet. 'Get your shoes on.'

She stared at him while her heart slowed its gallop. 'What?'

'Come on, Stuart. We haven't got all day.'

She did as he'd ordered, her eyes still on his. 'Where are we going?'

'To your camp.' She watched as he checked the safety catch, then tucked the pistol into the waistband of his jeans. 'How far is it?'

'You mean you're not...you won't—?'

He shot her an amused look as he retrieved the machete. 'I know this is going to come as a disappointment, sweetheart, but I've no designs on your body—delightful though it may be.'

She flushed. 'Then why did you follow me? Why did you sneak up on me? Why—?'

'Where are you camped?'

'Up the trail. But—'

She stumbled as he put his hand into the middle of her back and pushed her forward.

'Do you think you can manage to talk and walk at the same time?'

'I can even manage it without you poking at me,' Brionny snapped, twisting away from his prodding hand. 'How about telling me what's going on, McClintoch?'

'Ah, how quickly we forget our manners. A little while ago I was "Mister" McClintoch.'

'Dammit, McClintoch—'

'Do you know El Kaia Gorge?' Brionny nodded.

'Well, I'm with the construction crew that's surveying on the other side of it.'

'You mean you work for the company that's going to build that road?' Her face registered distaste. 'I might have known.'

Slade's eyes narrowed. 'What's the problem, Stuart? Do people who put in an honest day's labor offend your delicate sensibilities?'

What offended her sensibilities was the thought of a road through the jungle, but there was no reason in the world to explain herself to this man.

'If you work on the far side of the gorge,' Brionny said coolly, 'then what were you doing crossing it?'

'Sorry, lady. If you folks had a "Keep Out" sign posted, I didn't see it.' His smile thinned. 'All I saw was an arrow, shot into a tree on the trail ahead of me.'

'Such poor aim,' she said sweetly. 'What a pity.'

'It wasn't poor aim at all,' he said, giving her another little shove. 'It was deliberate. The arrow was a warning.'

'Well, of course it was. Somebody was telling you they don't like the idea of that road, McClintoch. Surely you can—'

'It was a Mali-Mali arrow.' He flashed her a cool smile. 'Maybe you've heard of them.'

'I've heard of them.' Certainly she'd heard of them. Hadn't she just helped Professor Ingram make off with their fabled treasure?

'Then you also know they're not a tribe to fool with. They're tough and dangerous.'

'Don't be silly. They're just secretive and—'

'They're also headhunters—or didn't your guide bother mentioning that?'

'They used to be headhunters,' Brionny said, giving

him a pitying look. 'There's no proof at all that they
still—'

'Listen, I'm not going to get into a debate here, Stuart. The point is they're angry about something.'

'Of course they are. Your road. Why else would they
shoot at you?'

Slade grabbed her arm. 'Be quiet!'

'Why? Because I'm saying something you don't want
to—'

She gasped as he clamped his hand over her mouth
and drew her back against him.

'Look,' he said, his lips against her ear.

Brionny looked. She saw the campsite just ahead, and
Professor Ingram still sitting at the foot of the tree, his
notebook in his lap.

'So?' she said, around Slade's fingers, her voice au-
tomatically dropping to the same whispery level as his.
'I don't see—'

'I don't either. Where are the other tourists?'

'What tourists? There's just the professor and me.'

'The professor and...' He groaned. 'No. You can't
be.'

'Can't be what?'

'Are you saying you're the archaeologists searching
for the Eye of God?'

Brionny went very still. 'How do you know about
that?'

'Don't answer a question with a question,' he said
irritably. A woman. And an old man, he thought, staring
at the professor's white hair. 'Didn't you people at least
have the brains to hire native porters and guides?'

'We're not fools, McClintoch. We have seven men
who—'

Who weren't there any more, she thought, staring at

the campsite. Where was everybody? When she'd left the cook had been preparing lunch, while the other men talked softly among themselves.

'Stay here.'

Slade's voice was low and taut with command. Brionny opened her mouth, prepared to tell him she didn't take orders, but then she thought better of it. Something was wrong. Very wrong. No sign of the guides, no sounds, no movement...

The hair rose on the back of her neck. Professor Ingram hadn't stirred in all the time they'd been watching him.

She watched as Slade circled the little camp, then carefully made his way into it. He squatted down beside the professor. After a minute he rose to his feet and turned to her, but by then she understood.

'He's dead, isn't he? she said, her voice quavering a little.

'Yes,' Slade said bluntly. 'From the looks of him, I'd say he had a heart attack.'

Brionny let out her breath. 'Then, it wasn't—he wasn't—'

'No. Your professor died a natural death.'

She nodded. It all added up. The way Ingram had looked the past months, the bouts of weakness he wouldn't admit to...

She swayed unsteadily. Instantly Slade was beside her, his hands clasping her shoulders.

'You're not going to be sick on me,' he said sharply.

Brionny swallowed and looked up at him. 'I know it's beyond you to understand,' she said shakily, 'but some of us have human emotions. I can't help it if I—'

'Yes. You *can* help it.' His hands tightened on her, and now she saw something in his eyes she could not quite identify. 'Look around you, Stuart. The professor's dead from natural causes. But nothing else is natural here. Your Indians are gone. Your stuff's been rifled.'

'Rifled?' she said, staring at him.

'Rifled,' he said flatly. 'Take a look.'

He was right. Her backpack lay open on the ground, the contents strewn around it. The professor's pack had received the same treatment, and their storage boxes had been torn apart.

'But—but who would do such a thing? And why?'

Slade's eyes bored into hers. 'Someone who wanted something you and the professor had.'

'Our supplies? But they're still—'

'The Eye of God.'

Brionny's heart thumped. That was twice he'd mentioned the Eye. Was that what had brought him here? Had he come looking for the expedition that had gone after the emerald?

Her gaze skittered past Slade to where a dozen tin cans lay spilled across the ground. The tea canister that held the emerald lay undisturbed. It was a good place to hide the stone, Ingram had said. No one would think to look for it there.

'Well?' Slade's voice was harsh. 'Aren't you going to check and see if whoever did this took your precious stone?'

Brionny looked into his eyes. They were the same color as the emerald and just as cold. Her heart thumped again but she spoke calmly.

'How could they,' she said, 'when we never found it?'

Slade's mouth narrowed. 'You're telling me the emerald wasn't in this camp?'

She nodded. 'That's right. We looked for it, but we didn't find it.'

'Then why did your men take apart your stuff and then run off?'

Brionny shrugged. 'The porters probably got scared when they realized what had happened to Professor Ingram. They're very superstitious, you know. And they probably went through our stuff to see if there was anything worth taking before they—'

'Doesn't that strike you as odd? Doesn't it worry you a little, Stuart?'

It did, but not half as much as finding herself alone in the jungle with a relic worth a fortune and a man with no scruples.

'What worries me,' Brionny said calmly, 'is how I'm going to get back to Italpa without a guide.'

Slade gave her a long, searching look. 'You're right,' he said. 'Getting out of here is our first priority. Pack up whatever you need and we'll get moving.'

She turned away and picked up her backpack. The tin tea box. She had to get to it without Slade seeing her.

'Do you know the way back to the river?' she said as she moved slowly across the campsite, mindlessly picking things up, stuffing them into the pack, her eyes never leaving the tea box.

'Heading for the Italpa would take too long. We'll backtrack on my trail, then cross the rope bridge at the gorge. There's a radio at the construction site; we'll call for a 'copter to come and get you.'

Would he take her safely to the construction site? Yes, why not? So long as he thought she'd found nothing, he'd probably be eager to get her out of here so he could come back and set out on his own search.

'Fine,' Brionny said. She glanced over her shoulder. Slade had grabbed a shovel from the expedition's equipment and was digging into the spongy soil. Quickly she reached for the tea box and dumped it into her pack. 'Well,' she said briskly, 'I'm ready.'

'Grab something to dig with, then, and give me a hand.' He looked up as she came toward him. 'We've got to bury your professor before the animals find him.'

Brionny shuddered as she reached for a trowel. 'Are you always this blunt, McClintoch?'

He grinned. 'Not to worry, Stuart. A stroll through the jungle, a trot across the bridge, and you'll have seen the last of me.'

Four hours later, Brionny came stumbling out of the dense trees panting, her clothing stained with sweat. Slade was standing a few feet away. Beyond him she glimpsed a gorge so deep and endless that it made her stomach rush into her throat.

'My God,' she whispered, 'I didn't think…'

She turned away, telling herself this was no time to give in to her fear of heights, reminding herself that she had only to make it across the rope bridge and she'd not only never have to look at Slade McClintoch again, but she'd be on her way back to Italpa—wonderful, sophisticated Italpa—and then to New York, bearing the stone that would memorialize Edgar Ingram and put her feet firmly on the path of academic success.

'I don't believe it,' Slade said in a flat, strained voice.

Brionny blinked. 'Don't believe what?'

He reached out, caught her by the wrist, and dragged her forward. She threw a desperate look toward the yawning chasm at her feet, then stumbled back, her eyes clamped shut.

'Take a look.'

'I can't,' she said. 'I have acro—I'm afraid of—'

'I know what acrophobia means, Stuart.' His arms swept around her and he drew her back against him, lending her trembling body the hard support of his. 'Open your eyes,' he demanded.

She took a deep breath, forcing aside the dizziness as well as the incongruous thought that it came as much from being in McClintoch's arms as it did from the swooning drop before her.

'What am I supposed to see?' she said, her eyes still tightly shut.

'Dammit,' he said angrily. 'Are you blind? Look!'

She did—and her heart dropped to her feet.

The bridge that was supposed to cross El Kaia Gorge was gone. Where there should have been swaying rope, there was only endless, empty space.

CHAPTER THREE

THE GORGE was impossible, at least two hundred feet deep and surely twice as wide. Brionny's gaze flew across it. What remained of the bridge hung drooping down the opposite cliff wall, swaying delicately in the wind.

Her stomach contracted into a hard, cold knot. Instinctively she clasped Slade's encircling arms. Her fingers dug into his muscled flesh as she fought the wrenching nausea that heights had always inspired.

Slade drew her closer. 'Easy, Stuart.' Step by step, he moved her back until the yawning gulf was no longer at her feet. 'There's nothing to be afraid of.'

'I know.' She swallowed hard. 'It's—it's completely irrational, but—'

'But entirely human.'

Brionny tilted her head back, just enough so she could see his face. He was smiling, but the smile was without derision.

'We all have our flaws, Stuart.'

She forced a smile to her lips. 'Not in my family,' she said, only half jokingly.

Slade's brows lifted. 'Ah,' he said, 'you're descended from a long line of saints, hmm?'

She laughed. 'Not saints. Scientists.'

'And scientists don't have irrational fears?'

'Well, it's not logical. I mean, when you understand what causes those fears—'

'Bull. Who pumped you full of such garbage, Stuart? You're as entitled to be scared of the shadows under the bed as the rest of us.'

The upside-down philosophy surprised her. Slade McClintoch was muscle and macho, a man who'd surely never been afraid of anything in his life, yet he was assuring her that it was OK to be exactly that.

'Anyway,' he said, 'I can make you forget your phobia.'

'You can?'

'Sure.'

'How?'

He smiled. 'Like this,' he said softly, and kissed her.

The kiss took her by surprise. There was no time to think; there was time only to feel the warmth of his lips and the answering warmth spiraling through her blood—and then sanity returned.

Brionny pushed him away. 'What are you doing?' she demanded.

Slade grinned. 'I told you. I'm helping you deal with your fear.'

'That's pitiful!'

'Really? I haven't had any complaints that I can remember.'

Her chin rose. 'Truly pitiful—that you should have to get your women by taking advantage of them in their worst moments.'

If she'd thought to insult him, she'd failed. He grinned again and shrugged.

'You know what they say. Whatever method works.'

'Well, this method's worked one time too many. Don't try it again.'

The grin faded from his lips, was replaced by a swift and dangerous smile.

'Threats, Stuart?' he said softly.

Brionny forced her gaze to remain locked with his. She was in no position to threaten him and they both knew it, but backing down would be an error.

'Promises, McClintoch. We'll be out of this place eventually. And when we are—'

He laughed. 'What will you do? Report me to the authorities for saving your pretty tail yet one more time?'

'You haven't saved anything yet,' she said coldly. 'Or have your forgotten that we're standing at the edge of El Kaia Gorge—with absolutely no way to cross it?'

Her taunt hit home. There was pleasure in seeing the self-satisfied grin wiped from his face—but no pleasure at all in suddenly reminding herself of what she had, for a few minutes, managed to forget.

'Yeah.' Slade nodded. 'Let me take a look at what's left of that rope.'

She watched as he walked to the rim of the gorge, held her breath as he squatted down, grasped the short, swaying end of the rope, and drew it to him.

'Dammit,' he said softly.

'What's the matter?'

'I was right.'

Brionny took a hesitant step forward. 'About what?'

'The rope's been cut!'

'Couldn't it have just come apart?'

Slade looked at her as if she'd suggested the bridge might have been carried off by space aliens.

'Of course,' he said coldly. 'Between the time I crossed it this morning and now, all those heavy hemp strands got together, had a meeting, and decided they'd dissolve their partnership. Why didn't I think of that?'

'There's no need to be sarcastic, McClintoch. My explanation is at least as reasonable as yours.'

He waved the end of the rope at her.

'Do you see this?'

Brionny glanced at the rope, then folded her arms over her breasts. 'So?'

'So,' he said through his teeth, 'rope that comes apart by itself doesn't do it with such neat precision.'

She looked at the rope again. 'Neat' was the word for it, she thought. It had been severed as cleanly as a loaf of bread.

Her eyes flew to his. 'But—but who would—?'

'The "who" is easy.' She tried not to shudder as he flung the rope back over the cliff and stood up. 'The Mali-Mali.'

'You can't be sure of that,' Brionny said quickly.

'No.' He shot her a quick, mirthless smile. 'I can't be sure. Hell, can you imagine such poor manners? Whoever did this didn't even leave a calling card.'

'There's no reason to be snide, McClintoch.'

'No. And there's no reason to stick your head in the sand. Someone cut the ropes, and we don't have a long list of suspects.'

'I know that. But there's still no reason to assume—'

He swung toward her, his eyes filled with anger. 'You and Ingram found the stone, didn't you?'

Brionny blinked, 'What—what stone?'

His mouth twisted. 'Don't play games with me, lady. You know damned well what stone. The emerald. You and the old man found it, you took it, and the Mali-Malis want it back.'

'That's not true! I mean—I mean, we didn't take it.
I told you, we didn't find it.'

'And that's still your story?'

'It's not a story. It's the truth. And you're wasting
your time, McClintoch. You're trying to shift the blame,
but you can't.'

'Me? Shift the blame?' He jammed his hands on to
his hips. 'For what?'

'If—I repeat if—the Mali-Mali really are angry, it's
at you. It was you they shot at.'

'I was a handy target. One outsider's the same as
another as far as they're concerned.'

'So you say. But *you* were the target, not the professor and me.'

'The operative word is "were". Taking out the
bridge puts us on an equal footing.'

'What do you mean?'

'What's the matter, Stuart? Can't your highly trained,
upper-class brain process this information? Let me sim-
plify it for you. The bridge is gone. We're stuck here,
on this side of the gorge, while the Mali-Malis decide
what they want to do next.'

Brionny stared at him. 'But—surely there's something we can do?'

Slade walked slowly to the rim and stared across it.
'So near and yet so far,' he said softly. 'The construction camp is only a couple of hours' walk.'

A couple of hours, Brionny thought, her gaze following his. A handful of miles to a field telephone, to civilization, to whoever was in charge of the company
where Slade McClintoch worked, where he'd probably
first heard about the easy pickings across the gorge,
about the archaeologists who'd come after the fabulous
emerald.

'Won't the construction company send someone after you when they realize you're missing?' Brionny felt a surge of hope. Why hadn't she thought of it sooner? 'They'll see that the bridge is out and—'

'No one knows I crossed El Kaia.'

'Someone must. Your boss. Your crew chief. Whatever the man in charge is called.'

Slade looked at her. This was the time to tell her that the man in charge was called Slade McClintoch...

No, the devil within him said, don't do that. Let the lady sweat a while; let her stop looking down her pretty nose at a man she obviously thinks is only slightly better than dirt.

He shrugged lazily. 'I didn't check with anybody before I took off.'

Of course, Brionny thought, she should have known better. Men like him came and went, taking jobs for a few days, walking off when they tired of the work.

'You'll be missed, though,' she said, trying to keep the desperation she suddenly felt from her voice. 'Somebody's bound to realize you're gone and—'

He shot her a pitying smile. 'Give it up, Stuart. No one keeps tabs on me.'

He turned away, jammed his hands into his pockets, and paced along the rim of the gorge.

'Damn,' he said, 'damn, damn, damn.'

'What about repairing the bridge?' Brionny said, more sharply than she'd intended. 'Is there a chance of that?'

Slade looked at her and laughed. 'Can you fly?'

'I already told you, McClintoch, there's no point in being sarcastic.'

'Then try using your head. How can we fix a bridge we can't reach?'

Her gaze flew over the wide chasm again. He was right. The bridge might as well have been on the moon.

'Well, what did people do before the bridge was here?' Slade gave her a look that made her bristle. 'Don't look at me that way,' she snapped. 'I know something about the history of this place, McClintoch. People from both sides of El Kaia have traded back and forth for centuries. Surely they didn't always have a bridge to walk across?'

'Yeah.' He smiled slowly. 'I suppose that's true. Hell, maybe you're not as useless as I thought.'

'Intelligence is never useless,' Brionny said coldly, 'but I wouldn't expect someone like you to understand that.'

Slade's smile narrowed. 'No. No, you're quite right. The only things I understand are sweat and hard work. All the rest is just so much garbage.'

'What a charming philosophy. I just— Hey. Hey!' Her voice rose as Slade bent down, grasped an end of rope, and began to ease himself carefully over the rim. 'What are you doing?'

'Putting my muscles to use. As you just pointed out, it's all I'm good for.'

He grunted softly as he began lowering himself. Brionny saw his muscles strain and expand under the soft, clinging cotton of his T-shirt. A rush of heat blazed through her blood. Vertigo, she thought, and looked quickly away.

'What's the matter, Stuart? I'm not going to fall, if that's what's worrying you.'

'The rope's not long enough to climb down, is it?' she said, ignoring the taunt.

Slade shook his head. 'Not by a long shot. But there's a narrow ledge ten or fifteen feet down—I can get that far. There might be something below it that I can't see from here, strong vines or maybe some footholds—'

'Footholds?' Brionny gave a choked laugh. 'Only if you're a mountain goat.'

'Yeah, well, I'm going to check it out anyway.' Slade squinted up at the sky. 'We've got a little time before it gets dark, enough to see if we have a shot at climbing out of here at first light tomorrow.'

'You're crazy, McClintoch. If you fall—'

'Oh, darling,' he purred, 'how sweet. I didn't think you cared.'

Brionny glared at him. 'Understand something. If you fall and break your head, I'm not coming down after you.'

He gave her a cocky grin. 'Ah, the sweetness of the woman,' he said. Clutching the rope carefully, he maneuvered down another foot. 'Come on, Stuart, think of how great it'll be to stand up there and say, "I told you so", if I go crashing to the bottom.' He looked over his shoulder, then shuddered dramatically. 'Just be sure you say it loud enough so I can hear you. It's a long way down.'

Brionny looked past him to the floor of the gorge. Panic clutched at her belly but she would sooner have died than let him see it. 'Go on,' she said, 'have a good time. There's no accounting for some people's tastes.'

She turned, marched to a mossy boulder, and sat down. With a display of elaborate unconcern, she slipped her arms from the straps of her backpack and set it at her feet. Then she unlaced one of her boots, took it off, and gently massaged her toes. When she looked up again, Slade had vanished from view.

Her shoulders slumped forward. Wonderful. She was stuck in the middle of nowhere with a man whose mo-

tives were suspect, and now he'd decided to play at
being a human fly. Was she supposed to pray he made
it down and back in one piece—or was she better off
hoping she never saw his face again? Sighing, she
jammed her foot back into the boot and laced it up. If
Slade was right a tribe of head-hunting Indians wanted
the emerald she carried in her backpack. If *she* was
right, it was Slade himself who wanted the stone. Either
way, she was in trouble.

She leaned forward and ran her hand lightly over the
nylon backpack, her fingers finding and tracing the faint
outline of the small metal box that held the Eye.

Only one thing was certain. She had the stone, and
she intended to keep it. She wasn't about to lose it, not
to a bunch of bloodthirsty savages or to a conniving
adventurer.

Professor Ingram had devoted years of his life to finding the Eye. She had been privileged to have been with
him when he'd finally achieved his goal. Now it was
her responsibility to deliver the emerald safely to the
museum, and that was what she would do.

She got to her feet, tucked her hands into the rear
pockets of her shorts, and tapped her foot. What was
taking so long? McClintoch should have been back by
now. She hadn't heard any yells or shouts of distress,
so he couldn't have fallen. Had he managed to find a
way to the bottom? Come morning, would he expect
her to sail over the edge the way he had, follow him
down, down, down…?

She shuddered. It was best not to think about that,
nor about what it would be like to claw her way up the
other side. Instead, she'd concentrate on what it would
be like once she was out of the jungle. She smiled. The

museum officials would be delighted. Her father would be proud. Her doctorate would be guaranteed...

Where in hell was McClintoch? How long could it take to see if there was a way to the bottom of the gorge?

She took a deep breath, then moved forward a few steps, trying not to think of the chasm ahead or of the man who might lie crumpled at the bottom of it. She didn't like him, but she certainly wouldn't want him to break his neck.

'McClintoch?' she said.

There was no answer. She frowned and took another couple of steps forward. Thickening shadows were beginning to crowd the gorge, turning it from a deep valley into a mysterious slash in the face of the earth.

A chill ran along Brionny's skin. She thought of the first night she'd spent in the rainforest, how nothing had prepared her for the blackness that had suddenly enclosed the campsite. Professor Ingram had looked across the glowing fire at her and given her one of his rare smiles.

'Incredible, isn't it, Miss Stuart?' he'd said.

It had certainly been that. The night had seemed like a living, breathing creature, one with a somewhat malevolent intent. She'd shifted her camp chair closer to a pool of yellow light thrown by one of the butane lanterns.

But there'd be no lanterns tonight. And if Slade didn't hurry, he wouldn't be able to see clearly enough to climb back up.

'McClintoch?' she said. The word came out a whisper, and she cleared her throat and tried again. 'McClintoch? Can you hear me?'

Dammit, where was he?

Something rustled behind her and she looked around, her eyes scanning the perimeter of the jungle. The trees seemed black, almost ominous. The sounds of the night were picking up now, the hiss and hum of insects mingling with the growing chirrup-chirrup of the tree frogs. Soon there'd be other noises too—the growls and grunts of the hunters, the shrill cries of their prey—

Brionny turned a furious face to the gorge. 'Dammit, McClintoch,' she yelled, 'where in hell—?'

A sudden, awful roar burst from the jungle behind her. Brionny screamed and swung around, heart hammering in her breast, then screamed again as a hand fell on her shoulder.

'Easy,' Slade said. 'Easy, Stuart. It's only me.'

She spun toward him. 'Where in God's name have you been?'

His brows lifted. 'That's a hell of a greeting.'

'Do you know how long you have been gone?'

'No.' He grinned. 'I forgot to take along a timer.'

Enraged, she struck out blindly, punching him in the shoulder.

'You bastard! Is everything always a joke with you?'

'Hey. Take it easy.'

'Why?' She punched him again, harder. Slade caught her wrists in one hand, imprisoning them against his chest. 'Why should I take it easy?' she said, her eyes flashing. 'Do you know what it was like to sit here and wonder if you'd fallen and broken your stupid neck?'

'Would it have mattered? You weren't about to come after me if I had. You made that clear, remember?'

'You're damned right I did! And—and it would have served you right if you *had* fallen!'

'Let me get this straight. Are you ticked off because I could have gotten hurt—or because I didn't?'

Brionny stared at him. 'I-I—'

He moved closer to her, still holding her hands in his. She could feel the slow, strong beat of his heart under her fingers.

'Well?' His voice was soft. 'Which is it, Bree?'

'Stop trying to reduce this to-to—'

'To logic.' He smiled. 'But you're a scientist. You pride yourself on logic, don't you?'

His eyes were fixed on hers. How green they were, how deep and smoky.

'You're—you're confusing me, McClintoch.'

'Am I?' He smiled, as if the possibility pleased him.

Brionny swallowed. What was happening to her? The heat of his body was becoming her heat; the hardness of it made her want to lean against him. Her eyes closed and she took a breath, inhaling his clean male scent, the faint musk of his sweat.

'Bree.' One of his hands slid up her throat, framed her face, tilted it up to his. 'Were you afraid I'd been hurt?'

She touched the tip of her tongue to her lips. 'I—I'm not inhuman, McClintoch.'

'Ah.' He nodded and touched his forefinger to the centre of her lower lip. 'That's nice to know.'

'And—and I didn't much relish the possibility of being left here alone.'

'I see.' The tip of his finger traced the seam of her mouth. 'In other words, given the choice between tolerating my intolerable presence and tolerating only your own, you'd sooner cast your vote for me.'

'Yes. No. Dammit, McClintoch, don't do that!'

'Don't do what?' His finger stroked across her lip again. 'This, you mean?'

'Please.' Was that hesitant voice really hers? Why

did it sound that way, as if she was asking for one thing but wanting another?

'Please, McClintoch—'

'Slade. My name is Slade. Don't you think we know each other well enough to be on a first-name basis?'

'We don't know each other at all!' she said, desperately trying to ignore the feel of his finger moving against her flesh. 'We don't—'

'Well, then,' he said, 'we'll just have to remedy that, won't we?'

He bent his head and kissed her, not as he had that first time at the Florinda, nor even the way he had a while before. This kiss had nothing to do with control nor even with passion. It was a soft, almost gentle kiss, the faintest brush of mouth against mouth, and yet Brionny felt as if she was being turned inside out, as if she might lift off the ground and float into the darkening sky.

Slade's arms went around her. 'Bree,' he whispered, and his mouth dropped to hers again.

'No,' she said, but what was the point? She was saying one thing and doing just the opposite, linking her arms around his neck, letting him gather her close. She whimpered as the tip of his tongue traced the path his finger had followed moments ago. His teeth nipped lightly at her lip and she sighed and opened her mouth to his.

'Yes,' he whispered, 'oh, yes!'

His hands cupped her bottom; he lifted her to her toes, drew her forward, and fitted her hips to his. He moved, rotating gently against her, and the world seemed to stand still.

'Please,' she whispered, just as she had a little while ago, only now she knew what she was asking him to do. He did, too. His hand slipped under her shirt. Brionny gasped at the heat of it, at the feeling of his fingers cupping her naked breast. His thumb brushed across her nipple, lightly, lightly—

A deep roar exploded from the jungle again, this time so close that it seemed to shake the ground they stood on.

It was like being doused with a shower of icecold water. Brionny's eyes flew open. She stared up at Slade, shuddered, then dug her fists into his chest.

'Let me go,' she demanded.

'Bree.' His voice was thick, the words slurred. 'Bree, listen—'

'Don't ''Bree'' me, you—you cheap opportunist!'

'What?'

'I warned you not to try this kind of thing again.'

His hands fell away from her. 'The return of the ice princess.'

'The return of sanity, you mean.'

He smiled tightly. 'Some day, sweetheart, that little hot and cold act's going to get you in deep trouble.'

'Just keep away from me, McClintoch. Can you manage that, do you think?'

'With pleasure,' he said coldly.

'I hope so, because the next time you try anything—'

'You're repeating yourself, Stuart, and anyway I haven't got time to listen.' He brushed past her and, before she could stop him. snatched up her pack and put his arms through the straps. 'Well?' What are you waiting for? Let's get going.'

'Get going where? Didn't you find a path down the cliff?'

'The cliff wall is absolutely smooth below the ledge.'

'Then—then what are we going to do?'

'What do you think we're going to do?' he said impatiently. 'We're going to retrace our steps, pick up the trail you and Ingram took coming in, and follow it back to the river.'

'That's impossible!'

'I couldn't agree more.' In the near-darkness, she could just see the look of disgust on his face. 'The thought of spending the next week with you doesn't thrill me, either.'

'Ten days,' she said, trying to keep her voice under control. 'Ten days, McClintoch. That's how long it takes to walk that trail.'

He shrugged. 'Have you got a better idea?'

Brionny put her hand to her forehead. 'There's got to be something else we can do,' she said, and all at once Slade could hear the desperation in her voice. 'There's got to be.'

He looked at her. The haughty, don't-touch-me look was gone. In its place was not just desperation but fear. She looked, he thought, as she had when he'd first seen her that morning in the lagoon—innocent and scrubbed and younger than her years.

For a moment he thought of taking her in his arms, of telling her that she didn't have a damn thing to be afraid of. He wanted to tell her that he wasn't the villain she obviously thought he was, that he'd never hurt a woman in his life and he sure as hell wasn't going to start with her. Most of all, he wanted to tell her that he didn't give a damn for the emerald he was certain she'd found.

But then he thought of the way she'd looked at him that night at the Florinda, of how she'd looked just moments ago, after she'd realized she'd almost come to life in the arms of a man like him, and his heart hardened.

'The only thing you can do,' he said, 'is make damned sure you keep up the pace—unless you want to stick around and see if that jaguar phones in his dinner reservation again.'

'Jaguar? Is that what...?' She took a deep breath. 'Then—then why are we heading into the jungle? Why don't we camp here for the night?'

'What a great idea, Stuart. Why didn't I think of that? We can stay right here, in the open, with the gorge at our backs so that if the jaguar comes to dine we have nowhere to run. Oh, and we can make things simple for the Mali-Mali, too. I mean, if it turns out I'm right and we're not on their popularity list, they can dispose of us the same way they disposed of that bridge.'

Brionny's eyes widened. 'You don't mean—you can't mean—'

'I noticed a small clearing on the way here. It wasn't much, but it's a lot safer than this.' He gave Brionny a quick, cool smile. 'Your choice, lady. You can tag along and take your chances with me or you can sit here and wait to see what strolls out of the trees first—the jag or the guys with the arrows.'

He turned without waiting for her answer and strode off into the jungle.

Brionny watched him go. Some choice, she thought bitterly. Slade had her pack. Her pistol. Her supplies.

And her emerald.

Oh, yes. It was one hell of a choice, but it was hers to make. Gritting her teeth, she set off after him.

CHAPTER FOUR

THE POSSIBILITY that Slade had lied, that he'd designed an elaborate charade for her benefit, didn't strike Brionny until they were half an hour into the jungle.

At first, she was too preoccupied with trying to match his stride to think of anything. Then, gradually, her legs found the right rhythm and she fell in behind him, near enough to reach out and touch him had she wished—which, of course, she had no desire to do—but not so near that she would be subject to any more lectures or commands.

'Don't fall behind,' he snapped, when she paused to fix her shoelace.

'Aye, aye, Captain, sir,' she said. 'Any other orders?'

Slade shot her a cold glare. 'Yes. I don't like women with smart mouths.'

He turned away and Brionny made a face at his rigid back. What he didn't like were women who couldn't be bullied. Or intimidated. Or scared out of their socks with stories about hungry jaguars and tribes of blood-thirsty headhunters.

And, just that quickly, it came to her.

Suppose he was lying? Not about the jaguar—she'd heard the cat's roar loud and clear, and anyway it was no secret that this stretch of virtually unexplored jungle was home to a considerable number of the big, handsome animals. But that stuff about being pursued by headhunters—what proof did she have that it was true? Yes, the rarely glimpsed Mali-Mali were rumored to have once been headhunters, but that was a long time ago. And it wasn't as if McClintoch had produced the arrow he claimed had been shot into a tree ahead of him on the trail.

As for the bridge at El Kaia Gorge—someone had cut it, all right. Someone had deliberately hacked the swinging ropes in two, probably with a machete.

Slade had a machete. He could easily have cut the ropes himself.

How long would it have taken to do the job? One minute? Two? He'd had plenty of time; she'd come straggling out of the trees at least three or four minutes after him.

He had asked her about the Eye of God and she had denied having it. Maybe he hadn't found her denial convincing. Maybe he thought she at least knew where the emerald was. It he wanted the stone badly enough—and she was certain he did—wouldn't he try almost anything to get information from her? Scaring the wits out of her, then making her totally dependent on him for survival, would be a damned good start.

Brionny stared up the trail. Slade was a dozen yards ahead of her now, his figure vivid in the bright moonlight, marching along as if he owned the world. A knot of rage ballooned in her chest. It was all too neat and tidy: the ravaging band of headhunters supposedly stalking through the jungle, the rope bridge destroyed by vengeance-driven savages... She'd bet everything that none of it was real, that Slade had invented the tale for her benefit.

The only thing she had to fear was him!

This morning she'd awakened in a neatly kept camp,

the junior member of a prestigious scientific team that had achieved the impossible. Now she was a second-class citizen, slogging along on the heels of a self-styled Indiana Jones who barked out orders and expected her to jump.

She might have the academic credentials, but Slade McClintoch had all the tricks—and all her resources.

Brionny glared at his steadily retreating figure. Her gun was tucked into the waistband of his jeans. Her backpack rode easily across his broad shoulders. He had everything of hers that would ensure survival in the jungle—not just the gun but the supplies in her pack, the bags of dried fruits and nuts, the water-purification tablets, the matches, the maps...

And he had the emerald. It was tucked inside the pack, just waiting for him to find. And when he did— when he did...

What unbelievable stupidity had made her stuff the Eye into a box of tea? A man searching for an emerald would go straight for it, just as she had when she'd sought a place to hide the stone. And then it would all have been for nothing—the professor's years of research, his death in the steamy jungle, her future—all of it would be wiped out.

Slade would steal the stone and take off. By the time she found her way to civilization—assuming she did— he'd be long gone, and the Eye would be in the hands of some greedy unscrupulous collector, traded for enough money to keep Slade McClintoch in whiskey or women, or whatever it was men like him wanted, for a long, long time.

Anger made her incautious. Marching along blindly, her mind crowded with unpleasant images and her blood pumping with fury, she didn't see the fallen tree that lay across the narrow trail. Her foot caught in a root and she tumbled to the ground.

Slade stopped and swung towards her as she scrambled to her feet.

'What's the problem?' he snapped.

'No problem,' Brionny shot back. 'Don't worry about me, McClintoch. I assure you I can take care of myself.'

'Am I to assume there's some deep meaning in that remark, Stuart?'

'I don't much care what you assume.'

He smiled tightly. 'You're pushing your luck, lady.'

'My luck ran out the night you and I bumped into each other in The Hotel Florinda.'

'Funny, but I've been thinking the same thing.'

Brionny dusted off her shorts. 'Then you ought to be more than happy to agree to my plan.'

'Let's hear it.'

She smiled brightly. 'You go your way and I'll go mine.'

'You really are a mind-reader, Stuart. As soon as we get to Italpa, that's exactly what we'll do.'

'I don't want to wait until we get to Italpa.' She strode forward and thrust out her hand. 'Give me my pack and my gun and I'll be on my way.'

'On your way to where, if you don't mind my asking?'

'Get that tone out of your voice, dammit! Do you think I can't find my way to the river? I have a map in that pack. I don't need your help, not for a minute.'

'That's not what you said when we found Ingram dead and the camp ransacked.' His voice rose in cruel parody of hers. '"What worries me is how I'm going to get back to Italpa without a guide"' you said.'

'I was in shock. I'd forgotten I had a map. And

you're the only one who thinks that camp was ransacked.'

He laughed. 'What'd they do, Stuart? Check it for souvenirs?'

'Stop trying to change the topic, McClintoch. I want my stuff, and I want it now.'

Slade gave her a pitying look. 'Don't be ridiculous. You wouldn't have a chance on your own.'

'Your concern for my welfare is touching, but—'

'Don't flatter yourself, lady. It's my welfare I'm concerned about. Two people have a better chance of making it out of here than one.'

'Meaning?'

'Meaning two sets of eyes and ears offer greater protection.'

'Against the bloodthirsty savages tracking us?' Brionny smiled coldly. 'I'll take my chances. Just hand over my things.'

'What have you got in this pack?' Slade demanded.

She felt her heart kick into her ribs. 'What do you mean?'

'Come on, Stuart, it's not a difficult question. What's in here? Food? Matches?'

'Get to the point, McClintoch.'

'We've got a ten-day walk ahead of us, a handful of resources, a map and a gun. Assuming I let you go off on your own—'

'Assuming you *let* me? Who died and made you king?'

'Assuming I did,' he said with airy disdain, 'how do you propose we split those things up?'

'Why should we split them up? They belong to me.'

Slade's eyebrows rose in mock disbelief. 'Where's your sense of morality? Are you saying you'd just watch me set off alone, without any supplies or weapons?'

'You're a big boy, McClintoch. You got yourself into this mess—you can get yourself out of it.'

He put his hands on his hips. 'Is this the same woman who told me she wasn't entirely without human feelings?'

Color flooded her cheeks. 'This is a ridiculous conversation!'

'Yeah. It is.' He settled the pack more firmly on his shoulders. 'Sorry, Stuart. Whether we like it or not, we're stuck with each other until we reach the river.'

'What you mean is I'm stuck with you,' Brionny said angrily, 'because you've requisitioned my supplies for you own use.'

'If that's the way you see it.'

'Is there another way to see it?'

Slade sighed. 'Even with a mountain of supplies and a gun in each hand, you'd never make it back to Italpa on your own.'

She looked as if she wanted to slap his face, Slade thought as he turned on his heel and set off along the trail again without giving her a chance to answer. Not that he cared. This wasn't about winning popularity contests; it was about survival.

Would she fall in line and follow after him? He smiled grimly to himself. Sure she would. She hated his guts, but she wasn't stupid. No matter what she said, she had to know he was right, that she needed him to make it back to Italpa.

He sighed wearily. On the other hand, she was dense as stone when it came to some things. The emerald, for instance. The Mali-Mali seemed convinced she had it, or had it stashed. He had no reason to doubt them. He didn't doubt the Indians' ability to keep them from reaching Italpa alive, either.

The messages had been easy to read. A trade, the Mali-Mali were saying. Free passage to civilization for the Eye of God.

Slade thought it sounded more than fair. The problem was convincing Brionny Stuart. Even after she'd seen what the headhunters had done to the rope bridge at El Kaia, she'd refused to tell him the truth.

But she would, eventually. It was just a matter of time. She was pigheaded and stubborn, but she wasn't dumb.

And, much as he hated to admit it, she was also beautiful. He liked his women in soft chiffon and delicate high heels, wearing discreet jewelry and smelling of Joy. Brionny Stuart was dressed in faded denim shorts, boots and an almost shapeless cotton T-shirt. She wore no jewelry, and the only things she smelled of were sweat and herself, and still she was sexier and lovelier than any woman he could think of.

His body tightened as he remembered that glimpse of her he'd had as she'd floated in the jungle pool, her hair drifting like yellow petals around her face, her breasts rising from the water like ivory globes tipped with the palest pink silk.

Dammit, what was wrong with him? He wasn't a boy, given to sweaty fantasies. He'd been busy as hell lately, yes, flying from one on-site emergency to another, but he hadn't lived like a monk. There'd been women. Hell, there'd always been women, attracted first to his muscles and then to his money. Heaven knew, there was nothing special about this one—unless you were turned on by snotty, ill-tempered bitches. Brionny Stuart had a cold heart and a sharp tongue and a grim determination not to tell him what she knew about the Eye of God, even if it meant that the two of them might end up as miniaturized *objets d'art* hanging on the wall of some Amazonian thatched hut—

'Ouch!'

He swung around. She was dancing from foot to foot, waving her hands in front of her face. Anyone who didn't know better would think she'd lost her mind.

'Mosquitoes?' he said, almost pleasantly.

The look she shot him was filled with fury.

'Of course mosquitoes,' she snarled. 'There's repellent in my pack, if you'd let me get at it.'

'Dousing yourself with bug spray once they start biting is useless. You should have done it hours ago.'

'Thanks for the advice. Now give me the bug spray.'

Slade shook his head. 'I don't want to stop now. You can use the stuff when we make camp.'

'And when will that be?' Brionny blew an errant wisp of hair from her forehead. 'If you figure on doing another million miles before then, tell me and I'll drop out now.'

'Keep your voice down.'

'I'm tired, I'm hungry, and I've given enough blood to the mosquitoes to win a medal from the Red Cross.'

'I said to keep your voice down.'

'Listen McClintoch, I don't know where you get this Genghis Khan complex from, but—'

She gasped as he caught hold of her shoulders.

'I get it from my basic instinct to survive,' he growled. 'You've got a pocket full of degrees—aren't you bright enough to figure out that you're making too much noise?'

'Sorry. If I'd known human speech would disturb your thought processes—'

'Have you forgotten about the Mali-Mali?'

'Oh. Right.' Brionny gave him a dazzling smile. 'The little men in grass skirts.'

'Actually,' Slade said coldly, 'they probably wear bark cloth.'

'Of course. Bark cloth. And plugs in their earlobes. And in their noses.' She shot him another bright smile. 'Just like in *National Geographic*.'

'Are you making a point?'

'Just that it's late, I'm tired, and I'm fed up being *smorgasbord* for the bugs.'

'I couldn't agree more.'

'Well, then...?'

'We'll stop when I decide we've put enough distance between us and anybody who might be following.'

Brionny nodded. 'The cannibals,' she said. 'Sorry. I keep forgetting.'

Slade's eyes narrowed. 'Come on, Stuart. You've spent snough time rubbing your academic credentials under my nose. What's with this sudden show of ignorance about Amazon tribes?'

'I'm just deferring to the man with all the information. That *is* you, isn't it?'

'I'm too tired to play games, lady. If you have something to say, say it. Otherwise, shut your mouth, grit your teeth, and hang on another few minutes. If I remember right, the place I figure on stopping at is just ahead.'

Brionny's eyes rounded with exaggerated surprise. 'A place the vicious headhunters won't know?'

'A place they won't find, if we're lucky. Anyway. I suspect they're more interested in tailing us for a while than in attacking.'

'How good of them to keep you informed.'

'Dammit, what's this all about?'

Suddenly she felt incredibly tired, too tired to go on with their verbal warfare. It had been a long, wearing day, and it wasn't over yet.

'Nothing,' she said. Sighing, she slumped back against a tree, slid down its length and plopped down on the ground. 'I need a breather, McClintoch. Just five minutes.'

He gave her a long, measuring look. Something that was a cross between admiration and pity welled inside him. He could see that she really was exhausted. Actually, that she'd managed to push this far was more than he'd expected.

'All right,' he said, after a moment. 'You sit there while I take a look around.'

Brionny nodded. 'Fine.'

He looked at her again. Her legs were drawn up and her arms lay limply across her knees. Her head was tilted forward so that the softly vulnerable nape of her neck lay exposed. There was a welt on her arm from a mosquito bite or a thorn, and he fought down the impossible urge to bend and put his lips to it.

Slade swallowed hard, forced himself to look away. The brush alongside the trail was a bramble-filled tangle. He could see a thick tree trunk rising perhaps fifty feet from where he stood. Was it the place he remembered?

He looked back at Brionny. She hadn't moved, except to let her head droop even further forward. That was how he felt, too, tired to the point of collapse. Neither of them could go much further tonight.

'Stuart?' She looked up. 'Will you promise to stay put?'

She laughed wearily. 'Do I look as if I could go anywhere?'

No, Slade thought, she certainly didn't. With a grunt, he dropped the pack from his shoulders.

'I'll be right back,' he said, and stepped into the bush.

The instant the dense foliage closed around him, Brionny sprang to her feet. Heart pounding, she pounced on the pack and all but ripped it open. She'd never dreamed she'd get lucky like this, that McClintoch would just drop the pack at her feet and walk off.

She hadn't lied about staying put. She was worn to the point of collapse and besides, she wasn't foolish enough to try and make a break for it at night.

But the emerald, she thought as she fumbled for the tea box, the emerald was a different story entirely. She could dig it from its hiding place, put it somewhere else.

But where? Her hand closed around the stone. Where could she hide the thing? It was only twenty or thirty carats in size, not huge, but bulky enough to—

Only twenty or thirty carats, she thought, biting back a gurgle of hysterical laughter, and only worth—what? A million dollars? Twice that? More?

'Stuart?' Brionny's heart leaped into her throat. She looked up wildly, her eyes sweeping the wall of brush. 'Stuart,' Slade hissed from somewhere behind it, 'do you hear me?'

'I hear you,' she said. Where to hide the emerald? *Where?*

'This place looks OK. Grab the backpack and come on through.'

Think, Brionny, think!

Swiftly she dug into the pack again. There was a package of tampons at the bottom. Her hands shook as she opened it, shoved the emerald deep inside, then closed it again.

She shut the backpack and was just rising to her feet as the bushes parted.

'What's taking so long?' Slade demanded.

Could he hear her heart trying to pump its way out of her chest? Brionny gave what she hoped was a lazy shrug.

'I told you, I'm tired. It took me a while to get myself together.'

She looked more than tired, Slade thought; her face was white with strain, her eyes dark pools of exhaustion—but whose fault was that? It was her fault they were on the run from a tribe of savages.

'My heart breaks for you,' he said coldly, 'but we've got more important things to worry about than you needing a night's sleep.'

'Forgive me, McClintoch.' Brionny's voice dripped with sarcasm. 'I keep forgetting. The jungle's alive with enemies. They're behind each tree, under each leaf—'

The breath whooshed from her lungs as he grabbed her and yanked her hard against him.

'This isn't a game,' he said harshly. 'And I won't permit you to act as if it is, not while you're playing with my life as well as your own.'

'You're right,' Brionny spat, 'this isn't a game! And I'm tired of pretending it is. Who are you kidding, McClintoch? The only thing we're in danger from is your over-acting.'

'Are you crazy, woman?'

'No.' Her jaw shot forward. She hadn't meant to tell him she was on to him, but what point was there in letting him go on playing her for a fool? 'And I'm not the impressionable jerk you think I am, either. This whole incredible story of yours, about the natives and—'

She cried out as Slade's hand whisked across her mouth. His arm went around her waist, inflexible as steel. In one swift movement he lifted her from her feet, jerked her off the narrow trail, and into the dense underbrush.

Branches tore at her hair; brambles raked her cheek. She kicked against his shins, yelled silently against his palm. Her teeth sank into his flesh, but though he cursed her under his breath he didn't let go.

And then, suddenly, she heard the sound.

A pulsebeat, deep and primitive, throbbed through the jungle.

She went still in Slade's arms.

'Do you hear it?' he whispered into her ear.

Brionny nodded frantically. His hand fell from her mouth and he drew her back with him through the bushes until they were standing in a small clearing. The drumming sound intensified, and Brionny turned without thinking and burrowed into Slade's embrace.

'Easy,' he whispered, while his hand stroked gently down her spine.

'What—what is it?' she said, her voice trembling.

'Our pals are sending a message.'

Of course. They were listening to the sound of hands drumming on a hollow log. How could she not have recognized it? A shudder went through her as she answered her own question. It was one thing to read about this ancient form of communication in a textbook but quite another to hear it yourself, in the humid darkness of a rainforest.

'It—it doesn't sound the way I expected,' she whispered.

Slade nodded. 'It never does.' His arms tightened around her. 'It goes right through you, doesn't it?'

Oh, yes, it certainly did. The drumming seemed to be all around them, defying her to tell where it was coming from. She knew only that it was the most primitive and frightening sound she'd ever heard. It was like listening to the heartbeat of some great, primordial creature, waiting out there in the darkness.

Brionny shivered again. Slade drew back a little, took her face in his hands, and lifted it to him.

'It it helps,' he whispered, 'I don't think it's the prelude to an attack.'

She made a sound that was supposed to be a laugh. 'Don't tell me. They're using Morse Code and you learned to read it in your days as a Boy Scout.'

He smiled. 'It wasn't such a hot idea to be Boy Scout where I grew up. Wearing a good guy's uniform was bad news in my neighborhood.'

Brionny pressed her forehead against his shoulder. 'Then how do you know what they're saying?'

'I don't. But if they wanted to rush us, they'd have done it by now.'

'Well, that's reassuring.' She looked at him again. 'So, what kind of message do you think it is it? "Dear Jane, I'll be late, don't hold dinner"?'

Slade laughed softly. 'Something like that.' His thumbs moved lightly across her cheekbones. 'I think they're sending out word that they know where we are, more or less, and that everything's under control.'

'Wonderful.'

'It is, when you consider the alternative.'

'An attack, you mean.' Brionny took a deep breath. 'You're sure they're not planning one?'

'I can't be sure of anything, Bree. But I can make a pretty good guess. The tribes I'm familiar with—'

'The tribes you're familiar with?'

He shrugged. 'I've traveled a bit through this part of the world and I've been in a few other places where primitive peoples still exist.'

Yes, she thought, looking at him, at the hard, masculine planes of his face, the sweep of dark hair, the proud yet sensual mouth, he would be a man who traveled in such places. He was a man drawn to adventure and the endless search for treasure, committed to nothing more than following the sunrise.

Why did the thought make her throat tighten?

Slade drew in his breath. 'The drumming's stopped.'

'I guess the telecommunications office shut down for the night,' Brionny whispered, trying for a smile to match the quip, but she failed miserably. Slade drew her closer.

'We'll be OK,' he said. 'They've had plenty of chances to hurt us, if that's what they wanted to do.'

'What *do* they want, then?'

The emerald, he thought, but somehow he couldn't bring himself to say it when she already looked so frightened.

'Maybe they just want to remind us that they're out there.'

Brionny stared at him. Was he telling her the truth? Or was he taking advantage of whatever set of circumstances had put that jungle drum corps within hearing?

She thought of that night at the Hotel Florinda, when he'd kissed her and the world had spun out from under her feet. She thought of the moment at the edge of the gorge, when he'd kissed her again and the taste of him had been more dizzying than the sight of the ground plunging away to infinity.

She barely knew this man; she didn't like him or respect the way he lived—and yet he was taking subtle control of her life.

'My God,' Slade said quietly. His eyes were narrowed, fixed to her face, and dark with sudden understanding. 'You think I made all this up, don't you?'

Brionny hesitated. 'Well, it's—it's all kind of—I mean, it's so strange, you know? The bridge, the arrow, and now the drums...'

He let go of her, so abruptly that she staggered back.

'The arrow came close enough to damned near part my hair. And you saw the bridge yourself; you saw the way the ropes had been severed. And those drums— what do you think, Stuart, that I've got a tape player in my back pocket?'

'No, of course not. I just—look, I'm trying to be completely honest with you, McClintoch. You can't blame me for expressing some doubts.'

'Doubts?' he said, anger and indignation sharpening his voice. 'Hell, lady, you're not expressing "doubts", you're labeling me a liar—and I damned well don't like it!'

Brionny stiffened. 'And I don't like having stories about headhunters and warning arrows and heaven only knows what else dropped on my head by a man who comes sauntering out of the jungle without so much as a how do you do!'

'My manners never were the best,' he said, flashing her a cold smile. 'Next time, I'll wait for a proper invitation.' He took a step forward, and Brionny fell back. 'Since you've got all this figured out, Stuart, why not tell me the rest? Why would I invent this whole elaborate story just for you?'

In for a penny, in for a pound, Brionny thought, and took a breath.

'It you thought I had the Eye of God,' she said, 'and if you wanted it badly enough, you might do anything to try and take it from me.'

Silence stretched between them, taut as a drawn string. Slade was still glaring at her, his broad chest rising and falling rapidly, and suddenly she knew that all he had to do was tell her she was wrong and she'd believe him. Not even the greatest magician could have staged the events that had been happening during the past hours. Everything was too well choreographed for one man to—

Slade snatched the backpack from the ground. 'You're wrong,' he said.

Brionny sighed. 'I believe you, McClintoch, and I'm sorry if—'

'I don't think you *might* have the emerald,' he said coldly. 'I'm *sure* you have it. And I'm not going to try and take it from you—I damned well *am* going to take it.' His mouth twisted in a smile that was not a smile at all. 'Any questions, Stuart? If not, I'd like to settle in for the night.'

CHAPTER FIVE

BRIONNY STARED at Slade, at the narrowed green eyes that were so coldly focused on hers. She felt a flutter inside her breast, a whisper of what might have been disappointment—but then Slade's lips curved into a self-assured smirk and she knew that the only thing she felt was overwhelming relief.

All the cards were on the table now. She didn't have to go on wondering if Slade was the villain in this piece or if he was her savior. He had identified himself for her, confirming what she'd suspected—that he was a man with the ethics of a snake and the determination of a pit-bull.

He wanted the Eye of God; he was sure she had it and he would do whatever it took to wrest it from her. Her only safety lay in steadfast denial that she had the emerald. It was her only protection against his stealing it and abandoning her in the jungle.

Slade was still smiling, that same damnably smug grin that made her yearn to slap it from his face. Instead, she smiled too, as if they were both in on some terribly amusing joke.

'Well,' she said, 'now that you've made your position clear, I suppose I ought to state mine. I'll make it easy for you, McClintoch, and put it in the simplest terms possible. I do not have the emerald. I have no idea where it is. But, I assure you, if I did, I'd sooner choke than tell you. Any questions?'

The smile disappeared from his face as he clasped her shoulders.

'Not a one,' he said with soft menace. 'But I do have an observation that might interest you. Keep pushing me and you may not like where you end up.'

'I don't like being threatened,' Brionny said coolly, despite the sudden frightened race of her heart. 'And I don't like being manhandled, either.'

'Manhandled?'

She dropped her gaze to where his fingers dug into her flesh. 'Manhandled,' she repeated in a frigid tone.

They glared at each other. The woman was impossible, Slade thought grimly. Her perfect little world was verging on collapse, but rather than admit it she'd decided to blame it on him.

'People like you amaze me,' he said. 'You go through life acting as if the world were created for you to command—and then you accuse the rest of us of not knowing how to behave.'

'On, give it up! The only thing you know about people like me is that if you hang around us long enough you might get a shot at stripping us bare.'

Slade laughed again, but now his laughter had a soft, suggestive sound to it.

'What a creative thought, Stuart. That's the best idea you've had yet.'

A wash of color rose under Brionny's skin. 'You know what I mean,' she snapped. 'You want something you think I have—'

'Damned right I do.'

'Face the facts, McClintoch. You're out of luck.'

'Back to square one,' he said flatly. 'You're going to keep insisting you don't have the emerald.'

'I can't help it if you don't want to deal with the truth.'

'Your story might impress me more if the Mali-Mali weren't after you—or do you think that band concert we were just treated to was for kicks?'

'Assuming you're right—if those were drums—'

'*If* they were drums?' He gave a bark of laughter. 'What else could they have been? Castanets?'

'If they were drums,' Brionny said firmly, 'maybe they were serenading you.'

'Me?'

'Come on, McClintoch. Don't sound so all-fired innocent.' She gave him a look that she hoped blazed with accusation. 'Remember that company you worked for, the one putting in the road? Maybe the locals don't like the idea of the jungle being desecrated.'

'Putting in a desperately needed road isn't a desecration. If you'd ever had the worry about getting to a doctor or a hospital or a decent school, you'd understand.'

'Slade McClintoch,' Brionny said, 'candidate for this year's Albert Schweitzer Fellowship Award!' She planted her hands on her hips and glared at him.

'What I don't want to be,' Slade said sharply, 'is Martyr of the Year. If you've got half a brain in that beautiful head, you'll take my advice. Give me the stone—'

'Hah!'

'Give me the stone, and I'll return it to the Mali-Mali.'

'Why, Mr McClintoch,' Brionny said, giving him a look of wide-eyed innocence, 'I've misunderstood your motives. You don't want the Eye for yourself. You want to return it to its rightful owners.'

'Dammit, Stuart! Will you stop being a fool?'

'You're the fool, not me, if you think I'm going to believe you're really Robin Hood in disguise.'

Slade stared at her, his jaw set, and then he grabbed the backpack from the ground and began yanking open the straps that kept it closed.

'What do you think you're doing?'

He sank down on a log, the pack in his lap. 'Figure it out, Stuart. What does it look like I'm doing?'

'That's my stuff,' she said, reaching toward him. 'You've no right to—'

He brushed her hand aside. 'Stop me, then.' He looked up, smiling tightly. His voice was soft as velvet, yet somehow rough with menace.

Don't react, Brionny warned herself; don't do anything.

She shrugged, as if the sight of him examining the contents of the pack weren't important.

Go ahead,' she said casually. 'Throw your weight around.'

Helpless to stop him, she watched as he sifted through her things. Her extra socks looked incredibly small in his hands. When he picked up a pair of white cotton bikini panties and looked at her, brows lifted, she didn't give an inch. 'My underwear,' she said coldly. 'I'd offer to lend, but I doubt we're the same size.'

Slade grinned. 'Let's see what else we have here that might be useful.'

'Just some stuff to eat and some personal things,' she said, with a show of disinterest. 'If you want something in particular, ask.'

'I already did. I want the emerald, remember?'

'Well, you won't find it here,' she said with more conviction than she felt.

'In that case, I'll just have to settle for whatever I—Aha!'

Brionny's pulse skittered. 'Aha, what?'

'Bug goop,' he said, tossing a plastic bottle to her. 'Better put some on before there's nothing left of you.'

She nodded, then sank down on the log beside him, watching with growing apprehension as he continued his hunt.

'What's this?'

'Penicillin tablets. The museum people thought it would be a good idea if—'

'This?'

'Aspirin.'

'What's in here?'

'An antibiotic. Honestly, McClintoch, if you'd just let me—'

'You've got a regular pharmacy here, Stuart. I'm impressed.'

'I'm delighted to hear it. Are you done messing with my property?'

'Well, well,' Slade said softly. 'And what have we here?'

Brionny went very still. He was holding the little tin tea box in his hands and looking at her as if he were a cat who'd found the key to the mouse hole.

'It's tea,' she said, when she could trust herself to speak.

'Tea?' He smiled gently. 'I thought there was nothing in here but personal stuff and first aid equipment.'

'Well—well, the tea is personal.'

'Do tell,' he said, very softly.

Brionny nodded. 'I like tea,' she said, her voice steady.

'Oh, yes, you must—if you were willing to carry your own supply instead of trusting it to one of the porters.'

'What's your point, McClintoch?'

'No point at all. I like tea myself.' His thumb toyed with the box cover. 'You won't mind if I open it, then, and take a sniff?'

His smile made a mockery of the polite request. You bastard, Brionny thought, you miserable bastard...

With one swift motion, he yanked the cover from the box and upended it in his lap. Tea leaves spilled out, trickled across his thighs, and fell on the ground. Slade looked down, then lifted his eyes to Brionny's.

'It's tea,' he said flatly.

'Yes.' She smiled sweetly, trying to still the race of her heart, trying not to think about how close she'd come to disaster. 'Did you expect to find something else?'

He glared at her, slammed the container shut, and dumped it into the pack.

'Are you satisfied now?' Brionny said. 'You've pawed through my things, acting as if you owned the wor—'

She swallowed. Slade was holding something else in his hands. It was the package of tampons.

Her mouth went dry. Say something, she thought fiercely; say something before he opens it.

'They're tampons,' she said briskly. He looked at her and she smiled coolly. 'Do you need me to explain what they are? Or would you rather dump the contents all over yourself so you can make an in-depth analysis?'

It was wonderful to see the quick flood of crimson that sprang out along his high cheekbones. His eyes dropped from hers. He looked at the tampon package as if it were liable to go up in flames, frowned, and tossed it into the pack.

'I thought you had something to eat in here,' he said gruffly, shoving the pack at her.

Casually, as if her pulse-rate weren't somewhere off the charts, Brionny nodded.

'I do.' She pulled out a couple of plastic containers. 'Nuts. And dried fruit. You get your choice.' She hesitated. 'Or do you want to spill it out and check to see if any of the raisins are emerald-green?'

Slade rose to his feet. 'I just hope you're still laughing when our drummer pals get tired of following us and decide to move in for a closer look,' he growled.

Brionny's eyes suddenly seemed very large in her pale face, and Slade almost regretted his sharp words. But then he looked past her, to the shadows surrounding the little clearing, and he knew the only thing worth regretting was Brionny Stuart's damned determination to hang on to her ill-gotten prize, even if it meant both their necks.

There wasn't any question in his mind now. The determination of the men following them, plus the woman's dogged declarations of innocence, had convinced him. She had the stone. But where? It wasn't in her pack. Was it, then, stashed somewhere on her?

He looked at her again. She was nibbling at the trail mix, bent on ignoring him. He watched as she lifted her hand to her lips. The tip of her tongue dipped delicately into her palm, and he felt his entire body tense.

What would it feel like if that tongue dipped into his mouth? Would she taste as he remembered, sweet and clean and fresh? Would she sigh and lean into him as she had the last time he'd kissed her; would she wind her arms around his neck so he could feel the softness of her body?

Damn! It was the emerald he wanted, not the woman. Where could she have hidden it? Did she have it tucked into a pocket or sewn into her clothing?

The only way to find out was to search her.

His breath caught, seemed to knot just in the back of his throat. He could imagine ordering her to stand, to take off that shirt that clung to her like skin, to peel off her shorts and underpants…

No. First he'd pat her down. Lift your arms, he'd say, and when she did he'd lift his too, he'd put his hands against hers and begin moving his fingers slowly along her skin, down her arms, her shoulders, to her breasts. He'd feel the weight of them against his palms, cup them while he watched her eyes darken as they had that night at the Florinda. Then he'd kneel before her, run his hands slowly over her hips and her buttocks, bring his fingers gently between her thighs while his thumb moved lightly against her.

Finally, when he had stroked every part of her through her clothing, he'd rise to his feet. Take your clothes off, he'd say softly, and he'd watch while she lifted her arms again and drew off her T-shirt, and when her breasts were free he'd bend and touch his lips to her nipples, draw them into the heat of his mouth…

Brionny looked up when Slade groaned. His face was pale, the cheekbones suddenly prominent as if he was in pain.

'McClintoch?' He didn't answer and she got to her feet. 'Are you OK?' She laid her hand lightly on his shoulder and he jumped as if she'd touched him with a hot poker.

'Let's go,' he snarled. He grabbed the pack and slung

it over one shoulder. 'We've wasted enough time on nonsense.'

So much for treating a rat with a show of kindness, she thought, and her lips curled with distaste.

'I was only asking if you were ill,' she said icily.

'Come on, Stuart. You'd be glad to see me collapse in a heap.'

Brionny's eyes snapped with anger. 'Yes, but it's probably too much to hope for. Well? What's your next order, General?'

'We make camp.'

'Where?' She swung in a half-circle, then stared after him. He was striding purposefully across the little clearing. 'Hey. Where are you going?'

The sniping had gone on too long, Slade thought wearily. He had one sort of enemy behind him and another sort beside him, and just now he was damned tired of both.

'To bed,' he said. 'I suggest you get your tail over here and do the same.'

'But—what are you doing?'

'For a woman with a bunch of fancy degrees, you certainly ask a lot of dumb questions. What does it look like I'm doing?'

He was standing beneath the branches of an enormous tree, gazing up into them as if he had all night to spend in contemplation of their leaves.

'I don't know,' Brionny said honestly. 'Is there something up in that tree?'

He laughed. 'You might say that, yeah.'

She tilted her head back, her gaze following his. 'I don't see anything.'

'Look again, Stuart. Right there—see? That forked branch maybe fifteen feet up?'

'So?'

'So,' he said, flashing her a quick grin, 'that's our hotel room for the night.'

She stared at him as the blood drained from her face. 'You're not serious.'

'I'm dead serious.'

She looked up. And up again. The tree was huge, taller and bigger in circumference than any she'd ever seen. It was something that might have sprung up after Jack had planted the magic beans.

Brionny took a step back. 'I am not going to climb that thing,' she said with conviction.

Slade sighed. 'I forgot. Your fear of heights.'

'Yes. My fear of heights. How good of you to remember.'

'Look at the tree, Stuart. Between the knotholes and the vines there are lots of places to grab.'

'Forget it, McClintoch. I'm not climbing that thing, and that's that.'

'You only have to make it to that forked branch. Once you get up there, you're home free. The branch is as wide as a sofa.'

'Forget it, I said.'

'Look, I know you're afraid—'

'I am not afraid.'

'You just admitted you were. And—'

'It's not a fear, it's a phobia.'

'Much more impressive. But I'm not interested in a discussion of phobias right now. I just want to see you get your butt up that tree.'

Brionny folded her arms. 'Well, you're in for a long wait. I'm not going to do it.'

To her surprise, Slade shrugged. 'OK. Have it your way. Sleep on the ground, if you want. It's your choice.'

She nodded. 'Exactly.'

'Just try not to make any noise, will you?' He brushed past her and gave the tree an assessing look. 'The wild pigs have sharp ears.'

'What wild pigs?'

'Of course, you can't do anything about your smell.'

'What smell? I don't—'

'They have such damned good noses. They can pick up a scent miles away.'

He's just trying to frighten me, Brionny told herself firmly.

'That's nonsense and you know it,' she said. 'Pigs won't—'

'Oh, and if you should hear any roaring—'

'Roaring?' she said weakly.

'We passed a stream a couple of miles back, remember? It wasn't very big but I'd bet it's got a fairly healthy caiman population. Once the frogs and the cicadas shut down for the night, you should be able to hear the big guys staking out their territory.' He smiled cheerfully. 'It's mating season.'

'I don't think—I mean, caimans don't—'

'Roar? Sure they do. They're like 'gators and crocs. Nobody's sure if they roar out of passion or because they're in a bad mood.' He shrugged. 'It's the rotten mood part you might want to remember.'

Brionny swallowed hard. 'None of this is true,' she said with determination. 'You're making it up to scare me.'

Slade grabbed a vine, put his foot on a knot of wood, and climbed a couple of feet before he paused and looked down at her.

'As for the jag—he should be done hunting in another couple of hours. With any luck at all he'll have found a capybara or two to fill his belly, and he won't be the least bit interested in you as an entrée.'

'I don't think this is funny, McClintoch!'

'Oh, by the way—if the guys who play the drums should stop by to say hello, don't wake me. I'm not much on conversation once the moon goes down.'

'Damn you,' Brionny said furiously. She stomped toward the tree, her face uplifted and angry in the waning moonlight. 'You win. I'll climb this miserable thing.'

Slade chuckled softly, dropped to the ground, and held out his hand. 'Ah Stuart,' he said, 'your eagerness to sleep with me is overwhelming.'

Flushing, she lunged at one of the tightly wound vines and began to climb.

'I hate this place. I hate you. I hate—' Her hand slipped, but before she could slide backward Slade caught her around the waist.

'Easy,' he murmured. 'Don't be afraid. I've got you.'

'And one fine recommendation that is,' she snapped.

But he did have her, his hands firm and steadying, his murmured reassurances helping to guide her, until, at last, she was sitting on the forked branch, trying to pretend the ground wasn't a million miles away.

'Relax,' Slade said as he scurried up behind her.

'I am relaxed. I am completely relaxed.'

'If you spend the night sitting like a statue, you'll be stiff in the morning.'

'Listen, McClintoch, maybe you can pretend this is a four-poster bed, complete with feather quilt and soft pillows, but I—' She gasped as Slade's arms went around her.

'Come here,' he said gruffly. 'Stop struggling, Stuart. There's nothing personal in this.' He laughed softly, his breath stirring the damp curls at her temple as he drew her back against him. 'Just think of me as your seat belt.'

'And what am I supposed to think about the branches above us?' she said, trying not to notice how closely she was plastered to the hard male body behind her. 'When you were having such a good time describing the wildlife on the ground, you forgot about the wildlife in the trees. How do you know there aren't snakes up here with us?'

Slade sighed. 'Do us both a favor and try and relax, OK? I promise you, we're safe. There's nothing to worry about.'

But there was, Brionny thought uneasily. There was the way it felt to be held so tightly in Slade's arms, with the beat of his heart against her back and the heat of him surrounding her.

'Will you loosen up, Stuart? Take a deep breath. Good. Now let it go.' He shifted his weight so that she was lying back in his arms. 'If you were really a hotshot scientist you'd know that a tense body falls at double the rate of a relaxed one.'

It was impossible not to laugh. 'What?'

Slade laughed too. 'You don't buy that, huh?'

'You must have slept through general science, McClintoch.'

He smiled. 'Something like that.' What was the point in telling her that he'd slept through most of his high school science courses because practical experience had by then taught him at least as much as any of his teachers knew? 'Just take it easy. You're not going to fall.'

'My head agrees. But my stomach doesn't. It's doing loop-the-loops at the thought of being up this high.'

'You flew to Peru, didn't you?' Brionny nodded.

'Well, how did you manage to survive the flight? Tranquilizers?'

'No. I don't like taking stuff like that.' She hesitated. 'It'll sound silly—'

'Try me.'

'Well, I made myself fall asleep. It's what I always do when I'm up in a plane.'

'You make yourself fall asleep?'

'I told you it would sound silly,' she said defensively. 'But it works.'

'How do you do it?'

She sighed. 'I tune out my surroundings. You know—I pull down the window shade so I can't see out, I get the flight attendant to bring me one of those little pillows so I can put my head back, I burrow under a blanket, and I tell myself I'm really not up in the air but that I'm—' She made a little sound of distress as Slade turned her in his arms. 'What are you doing?'

'I'm putting you across my lap,' he said in a no-nonsense voice, 'and there's no point in complaining because, believe me, I'm only doing it for our safety.'

Brionny felt the heat of his body encompass hers. Her nose brushed his cheek; her hand slipped across his chest.

Safe, she thought. Safe?

'That—that makes no sense. There's no reason to—'

'There's every reason,' he said firmly. 'If you don't get any rest, I won't either. And tomorrow we'll both need our wits about us.'

'Yes, but this—'

'Look, we don't have a window shade to pull down, nor a pillow. But you can put your head against my shoulder and close your eyes.' His hand came up, his fingers warm as they tunneled into her hair, and he brought her cheek to his chest. 'Now. Where shall we pretend we are? Do you have any preferences?'

Brionny gave a little laugh. 'Anywhere but a mile up in a tree.'

'OK. I've got it. It's summertime, and we're sitting on my aunt Bessie's wooden swing.'

'Come on, McClintoch—'

'The swing is very old. And it needs to be oiled. It creaks when it moves.'

'Look, I appreciate what you're trying to do, but it won't—'

'The moon is up.' Slade's voice whispered against her skin. 'It's a warm night, and the wind's coming in soft and easy from the south. We've been sitting out here for hours, just talking and counting the stars. Now we're both getting sleepy. "I'm tired, Slade," you say, and I say, Well, why don't you just put your head on my shoulder and close your eyes?'

'McClintoch, really. This is interesting, but—'

'A second ago you were calling me Slade.'

'No, I wasn't.'

'Sure you were. "I'm tired, Slade," you said, and I told you to put your head down and close your eyes.'

She couldn't help smiling. 'Nice try, but that wasn't me talking, it was you, speaking for me.'

'Me? Putting words in your mouth?' He smiled too, and drew her closer. 'Come on, give it a shot. Put your head on my shoulder, take a deep breath, and relax.'

With a little sigh, she did as he'd asked. Amazingly enough, she felt the tension begin easing from her body. Gradually she became aware of Slade's scent, sweaty and male. And exciting—but how could that be? What on earth could be exciting about the smell of sweat?

The way he was holding her was exciting too. She

had never imagined feeling so safe in a man's arms—
and yet feeling so aware of herself as a woman. Her
skin felt so sensitized, and so hot where his touched it.

Her hand lay against his chest, her fingers lightly
curled into the damp cotton of his shirt. His cheek was
against her temple. He needed a shave, she thought suddenly; she could feel the faint abrasion of his shadowy
beard against her skin. What would happen if she put
her hand to his cheek and let her palm play softly over
the light stubble? Her heart gave a thud, then another,
and she shifted a little in Slade's arms.

'Comfortable?' he whispered.

Brionny nodded, although that wasn't quite the way
she'd have described how she felt. Slade's throat was
inches from her mouth. What would his skin taste like?
she wondered. And his lips—how would they feel on
hers? His kisses this morning had seemed as hot and
fiery as the sun. Now, with the moon slipping from the
sky and the blackness of night settling around them,
would his kisses taste of coolness and of the dark?

Brionny shut her eyes. She could imagine going
down into that darkness with Slade, letting him carry
her into a bottomless whirlpool where there was nothing
but him and the night and the feel of his body against
hers...

'Bree.'

She lifted her head and looked into his eyes, as deep
and green as the jungle. His hand stroked her cheek.

'You're tensing up again,' he said softly.

'This isn't working,' she said shakily. 'I think—'

'You're not supposed to be thinking.' His voice was
husky, but it sounded as if it was somehow shot through
with silver. 'You're supposed to be relaxing. That was
the whole point of this, remember?'

The truth was that she was having trouble remembering anything.

'McClintoch—'

His mouth brushed lightly against her temple. 'My name is Slade.'

She swallowed. 'Slade. Please—'

He smiled. 'I like the way you say my name,' he whispered.

Their eyes met again, and what she saw in his made the breath catch in her throat.

Slade murmured her name, tilted her face to his, and kissed her.

CHAPTER SIX

IF ONLY Slade had kissed her with passion, or even with anger—with any of the fiery emotions they'd sparked in each other since they'd met—Brionny knew she could have handled it. She could have shoved him away, slapped his face, done what women had always done to humiliate men who took advantage of a woman's momentary weakness.

But he was kissing her with a sweetness that was almost unimaginable. His lips moved gently on hers, silk against satin; his hands cupped her face, his thumbs gently tracing the delicate bones. An unpredictable kiss, she thought hazily, from an increasingly unpredictable man.

She knew the kiss was meant to be a distraction, a calculated assault on her senses to divert her from reality. And it was working, she thought as he drew her closer. She could feel her fear slipping from her, falling away into the night. The trouble was that something just as dangerous was replacing it. Her mouth was softening under Slade's, her pulse-rate was quickening. Her hands were spreading on his chest, her fingers curling into his shirt.

With a little moan, she twisted her face from his. She waited, struggling for composure. When she thought she'd regained it, she looked at him and managed a strained smile.

'Thank you,' she said, as if he'd given her some aspirin for a headache. 'I'm OK now.'

Slade stroked damp tendrils of hair back from her temples. 'You're not afraid?'

'No, not any more.' She smiled again, a little less tremulously. 'Your diversionary tactic worked. I feel much calmer.'

It wasn't true. She felt anything but calm. He was tracing the lobe of her ear, his finger moving lightly along the tender flesh, and, though she'd tried to put some distance between them, how much distance could you manage when you were sitting in a man's arms?

His fingers dropped to the neck of her T-shirt and traced a path that encircled her throat.

'Do you?' he said softly. 'Feel calmer, I mean.'

'Absolutely.' Brionny cleared her throat. 'And you were right about this branch. It's so wide that I can't possibly fall.'

'No, you can't.' He looped both arms around her. 'I'd never let it happen.'

His arms were a strangely welcome fortress. It took effort not to lean back in his embrace.

'In fact,' she said, 'I—I don't even feel woozy about being so high.'

Slade chuckled. 'All that reassurance from one kiss? I'm flattered, Stuart.' His smile tilted, grew soft and lazy. His gaze dropped to her mouth. 'Just think how reassured you'd feel if I kissed you again.'

'No,' she said, her voice breathy and high-pitched. She cleared her throat again. 'I mean—it's not necessary. Really.'

'It's OK,' he said solemnly. 'I'm willing to make the sacrifice.'

Her eyes flashed to his. 'Don't make fun of me,' she said sharply.

'Me? Make fun of you?' He wore the angelic expression of a choir boy with a frog tucked in his back pocket. 'I wouldn't do that.'

Brionny ran the tip of her tongue over her lips. Was he flirting with her? If he was, he was wasting his time. She wasn't into that kind of male-female banter, not on the ground and certainly not here, in the branches of a tree in the Amazon with a man like Slade McClintoch.

He touched his forefinger to her mouth, drawing it gently along the curve of her lips, leaving a trail of fire in its wake.

'I was just thinking, Stuart...an experiment always has to be repeated before it has validity. Isn't that right?'

'If you expect me to find that amusing—'

'I expect you to treat this with scientific detachment.' He laid his finger against her lips again. A tremor went through her as he began to trace their outline. 'Such a sweet mouth,' he whispered. Her lips parted slightly. His fingertip slid inside and moved gently over the damp inner flesh. 'Just think of this as our treehouse lab,' he said. He was still smiling, but his voice had grown thick, the words softly slurred. 'I have no personal stake here. It's all in the interest of science.'

'It isn't. You know it isn't. And—and—' She caught hold of his hand as if she were catching hold of reality before it slipped away completely. 'Slade. You aren't listening.'

'Of course I am.' His fingers curled around her wrist. He lifted her hand to his mouth, pressed a kiss against the palm. 'I'm listening harder than you can imagine.'

'You're not,' she said, trying not to tremble at the feel of his lips against her skin.

'Of course I am.' He turned her hand over, kissed the inside of her wrist. There was no lightness in his voice now, no teasing tone at all. 'I'm listening to everything, sweetheart, even to the things you're afraid to say out loud.'

'You're talking nonsense,' she said shakily. 'Slade, please, you have to stop.'

A murmuring sigh of pleasure whispered from her lips as he kissed her.

'Is that what you really want me to do, Bree?'

Her head fell back as he pressed his mouth to her throat. What *did* she want? Not this, she thought desperately. Surely not this. Even if Slade wasn't lying about the headhunters—and that was a damned big 'if'—he was still the sort of man she knew better than to trust, a man dropped into her path by a fate with a bad sense of humor...

But what happened to all that logic when he kissed her?

'Tell me what you want,' he whispered, but it wasn't really a question for he was already kissing her deeply, hungrily, and she was kissing him back.

Her lips parted and his tongue slid against hers. He tasted like spring mornings and summer rain, like the first cool snowflake dropping from a winter sky. He tasted of fire and of flame, and when he drew up her shirt, baring her skin to the soft night air and to his caresses, Brionny moaned against his mouth. Heat pooled between her thighs as his thumb rolled across her nipple.

'Slade,' she whispered, 'Slade, please...'

He groaned, lowered his head, put his mouth to her

breast. His tongue laved her skin, and she cried out as his teeth closed lightly on the aching nub of flesh. He drew it into the warmth of his mouth and she felt her last hold on reality slipping away.

What was happening to her? She had never felt like this before. Hers was a world of cool scientific thought and careful investigation. There was no room in it for madness—and surely what she felt now was madness. Pull back now, she thought desperately; pull back before it's too late.

Instead, her hands swept into Slade's hair. She grasped his head and dragged his face to hers, her mouth hot and open against his. He was trembling too— she could feel it—and the realization sent a lightning shaft of pleasure curling through her blood.

'You are so beautiful,' he whispered.

She was—but it was such a pathetic way to describe her that Slade almost groaned with despair. Words had never been his strength; he was a man whose thought processes ran to problem-solving, not poetry, and those rare times when mathematical formulae hadn't worked, muscle always had.

Now he cursed the moments he'd read Euclid instead of Shelley. A perfect sunset was beautiful, or a warm summer morning. But the woman in his arms was much more than that. She was everything female, as mysterious and as lush as the jungle that surrounded them, yet she had a clever mind, as agile as any he'd ever known. She had a face a man dreamed of, a body that was perfection. Her lips were soft and yielding, tasting of honey, and she had set him on fire. He burned as he never had in all his years; he knew that only the exquisite sweetness of her body closing around his could ease his pain.

He arched her back over his arm, touched the tip of his tongue to her nipple, and she made a strangled sound of pleasure that set his blood to pounding in his ears. He took her hand from his chest, stroked the palm with the tip of his tongue, then slid it under his shirt.

'Touch me,' he whispered.

Touch him. Oh, yes, Brionny thought, that was what she wanted to do. She ached to touch him, to explore the hardness of his body. She thrust her fingers into the soft mat of hair that covered his chest, danced them across the hard layers of muscle that were so hot beneath her hand. She stroked his flat, taut abdomen and then hesitated, wanting to touch him even more intimately but afraid to do it, afraid of this sudden, driving need that was so terrifyingly new.

Slade clasped her wrist, brought her hand down his body, over the straining denim of his jeans to his aroused maleness, and she gasped at his heat, at the power she had unleashed.

'Feel what you do to me,' he said thickly.

She knew what she did to him, knew what he did to her. But it was wrong. It had to be wrong—although at the moment she couldn't remember why, couldn't remember anything but the feel of being in Slade's arms.

'Wait,' she said urgently. She caught his wrist, stilled his hand against her breast while she fought for control. 'Please, Slade. We—we can't—'

'We can.' His voice was low, fierce with elemental need. 'All I have to do is—' He lifted her, brought her across his lap so that she was straddling him. He cupped the back of her head, brought her mouth to his and kissed her. He put his lips to her ear, whispering what he wanted to do to her.

The husky words sent fire racing through her blood.

When he lifted his knees, she eased back against his upraised legs, her eyes closed, her heart hammering, riding the hardness of his body, luxuriating in the feel of him against her and under her. Her hips lifted, moving instinctively to welcome that full male pressure.

His fingers moved against her shorts and the zipper hissed open. Slade spread his hand against her belly, his touch silken on her warm skin as it brushed lower and lower...

A roar rent the night. The sound was primitive and terrifying, and Brionny froze in Slade's arms.

'The jaguar,' she whispered.

'It's all right, sweetheart.' His voice was gruff, impatient. 'He's not going to bother us.'

She sat up straight, her spine stiff with tension. 'But where is he? He sounds so close!'

Slade cursed softly. Then he sighed, reached for her, and drew her into his arms. Brionny buried her face against his shoulder as he soothed her, his hand stroking gently against her back.

'The jag's made his kill by now,' he said. 'He's not interested in us.'

'But that roar—'

'It was a roar of self-satisfaction. The cat's no different from any other predator.' Slade smiled, pressed a kiss against her temple. 'He has what he wants, and now the world belongs to him.'

Brionny went very still. It was such a simple analogy—and such a humiliating one. The jaguar had made its kill—and Slade had almost made his.

He wanted the emerald—the emerald he was certain she had. He would do anything to get it—and, with her eager assistance, he almost had.

That was what this seduction scene had been all about.

God, how could she have been so stupid?

A taste as bitter as ashes filled her mouth.

'Let me go,' she said in a low voice.

'Sweetheart, trust me. There's nothing to be—'

'Trust you?' Brionny's voice rose. 'Trust *you*? I'd sooner trust a whole nation of headhunters!'

'Bree, I promise, the cat won't—'

'Damn the cat!' She pulled away from him, shifting off his lap and out of his arms, angry enough to ignore the drop beneath them as she scooted back along the branch. 'And damn you, Slade McClintoch! You're disgusting! I wish I could—I wish I could—'

'What?' His voice had gone cool and flat. 'What do you wish you could do, lady? Take back the last few minutes? Pretend you'd never lowered yourself to my level and trembled in my arms?'

'If I was trembling, it was only because—because I was forcing myself to endure—'

'Oh, yeah. Right. You sure as hell were "enduring" me, Stuart.' Anger at himself for wanting her made him cruel and reckless. 'That's what those little sounds you made were all about. That's why you were rubbing against me as if—'

'Don't be insulting, McClintoch! I went along with it just to see how far you'd go to get what you want.'

Slade's mouth twisted. 'Meaning I was making love to you so you'd tell me where you've hidden the emerald?'

'Making love? Is that what you call the way you were pawing me? Maybe it wows the belles in Italpa, but—'

Slade's hand flashed out and caught hold of her wrist.

'Don't push your luck,' he said. 'We're in the middle

of nowhere, and there's nothing that stands between you
and whatever's out there—except me.'

'You seem to have forgotten that whatever's out there
is following the both of us.'

She could see the chill flash of his smile, even in the
darkness.

'Ah, but that's only a temporary condition, isn't it,
sweetheart?'

'I'm not good at riddles,' she snapped. 'If you've
something to say—'

'It's simple, lady. I have your supplies. I have your
gun. And, sooner or later I'll have your emerald.'

'I've told you and told you, I don't have—'

'Skip the lies, Stuart. I'm going to get that stone and
when I do this little game we've been playing will take
on a new set of rules.' Slade let go of her and leaned
back into the forked branch. 'Is that clear enough?'

It was clear, all right. Once he got what he wanted—
if he got what he wanted—she'd be on her own.
Whether she got back to civilization or not would be
her worry.

It certainly wouldn't be his.

'Well?' Slade's voice was gruff. 'Don't tell me you
haven't got some kind of snappy comeback. If there's
one thing I've learned about you, it's that you've always
got to have the last word.'

Brionny's chin rose. 'There's no advantage in having
the last word over someone who's not up to the chal-
lenge,' she said coldly. 'I'm going to try and get some
rest. I'd appreciate it if you'd shut your mouth and do
the same.'

If her feet had been on the ground, she'd have pivoted
on her heel and marched off. Instead she did the best

she could, shifting her weight recklessly, swinging her leg across the branch, and turning her back to Slade.

She would ignore him for the rest of the night. She wouldn't sleep, of course. For one thing, her adrenaline was pumping like crazy, and then there was the fact that she was sitting in mid-air, with the ground an awfully long way down, something she'd somehow managed to forget until now.

Slade seemed to read her mind.

'If you try to sit balanced like that all night,' he said with a resigned sigh, 'you're almost certain to fall off.'

'Thank you for worrying about my comfort,' she said primly. 'But I'm fine.'

'You're perched out there like an acrophobic Humpty Dumpty, Stuart, which is pretty stupid when you consider that the whole idea of climbing up here was so we could relax and get some rest.'

'Your concern is touching, but—'

'Concern? Listen, lady, once we're out of here you can walk a tightrope across El Kaia Gorge, for all I care. But for now, while I'm in charge—'

'Put your mind at ease, McClintoch. You're not in charge. And I've no intention of falling.'

He laughed unpleasantly. 'Neither did Humpty Dumpty.'

'I can't possibly fall because I won't be asleep,' Brionny said, ignoring his puny attempt at humor. 'So you see—' She yelped as Slade reached forward, put his arms around her, and dragged her into his embrace. 'How dare you? Let go of—'

'Relax. I've no evil designs on your body.'

'Dammit, McClintoch! Let me go!'

His arms tightened around her. 'How can I steal the

Eye of God from you if you fall out of this tree and get eaten by a jaguar?'

'You said the jaguar was—'

'I know I did. But you can't believe anything a man like me says, Stuart, remember?'

'You won't get any argument from me,' Brionny said tightly.

'Exactly. Now, lean back against me, shut your eyes, and go to sleep.'

'Sleep? Like this?' She folded her arms over her breasts. 'You have to be kidding.'

'Well, I'm going to get some sleep. What you do is your business.'

'In that case, let go of me.'

'With pleasure, once the sun rises and we're on the ground again.' Slade tugged her unyielding body back into the cradle of his, then brought her head to his shoulder with a firm hand. 'Until then, you can sit here and count the ways you hate me.'

'There aren't enough hours in the night for that!'

'Or you can stop being an ass and relax.'

'It would be easier to relax with the jaguar.'

'I wouldn't wish you on the cat. Your claws are more lethal than his.'

'Honestly, McClintoch—'

'I warn you, Stuart, my patience is wearing thin.'

'Your patience? What do you mean, your patience? I'm the one who—'

Slade caught her chin in his hand, turned her face to him, and silenced her with a hard, swift kiss.

'Keep talking,' he said, 'and I'll just have to think of some other ways to shut you up.'

Brionny's hands knotted into fists. 'I hate you,' she

snapped. 'Do you understand? I *hate* you, Slade Mc-Clintoch!'

'Yeah.' He yawned, put his head back, and shut his eyes. 'I understand completely.'

'I hope so,' she said angrily, 'because—'

A soft, rasping sound purred from Slade's throat. Brionny stared in disbelief, then rolled her eyes to the sky.

Damn Slade McClintoch to hell! Wasn't it bad enough that she was trapped in his arms for the balance of the night? Did he have to snore, too?

She was just going to have to sit here and endure it. She wouldn't even be able to relax. Relaxing would be... She yawned, then yawned again. Relaxing would be—it would be—

Her head drooped against Slade's shoulder. She gave a deep sigh and fell headlong into sleep.

'Bree?'

'Mmm.'

'Bree. Wake up.'

Brionny sighed. What a strange way to have fallen asleep, she thought drowsily. She was half reclining against something unyielding yet incredibly comfortable; her arms were enclosing not her pillow but something warmer and far more pleasant.

'Sweetheart.' A voice whispered softly in her ear, stirring the tendrils of hair that curled back from her cheek. 'Bree, you have to wake up now.'

Slowly, her lashes lifted from her cheeks. In the early dawn light Slade's face was a breath from hers. He had a look on his face that was impossible to define, like a man caught midway between heaven and hell.

'Bree.' His gaze swept across her face. 'Bree, I want you to listen to me.'

How could she listen when she was trying to figure out how she'd ended up lying in his arms? With a flurry of limbs, she tried to put some distance between them but his hold on her was like steel.

'I might have figured you'd try and take advantage of me the one second I let down my guard! Just because I dozed off it doesn't mean you're free to—'

'You've been asleep the whole night,' he said, his voice low and humming with a strange kind of tension.

Brionny snorted. 'Don't be ridiculous. I'd never—'

'Listen to me, Bree.'

'Why? So you can invent more lies?' She slammed her fist against his shoulder. 'Let go!'

'Will you listen to me?'

'Get your hands off me first.' Slade muttered a word that made her cheeks turn scarlet. 'You have no principles at all, McClintoch. A man who has to resort to such subterfuge—'

She gasped as his mouth dropped to hers. She struggled wildly against his kiss. Then, slowly, she went still. Her breath quickened—and Slade took his lips from hers and pressed them to her ear.

'In a little while,' he whispered, 'we're going to have company.'

She drew back and stared at him, seeing for the first time the grim look in his eyes.

'The jaguar?' she said.

'No such luck,' he said, and hesitated. He could see doubt creeping into her eyes. She knew what he was going to say, and she didn't want to hear it.

Damn! Moments before, he'd heard the drums again, heard the change in their rhythm, and he was certain there was going to be an attack soon. Still, there was a possibility he could turn things around—if he could convince Brionny that he was telling her the truth.

But how? How could he change the doubt in those blue eyes to belief? It had to be done quickly. There was no time to waste on another round of argument.

There was one chance. He could do what Brionny was sure he'd been doing all along. He could lie, though he didn't much like the idea...

'I hope this isn't going to be another story about the Mali-Mali,' she said coolly, 'because if it is—'

Hell, Slade thought, lying to her was better than letting her sit here like a target in a shooting gallery.

'Listen to me,' he said. 'I don't want to frighten you, but I saw something a few minutes ago.'

She stared at him, eyes watchful. 'What?'

'Two of their scouts. They were out there, just past those trees.'

She followed his pointing finger. He could see the change coming over her face.

'Are you sure?'

Slade drew her closer, hating himself for what he was doing yet praying it would do the job.

'Positive.'

She nodded. 'At least we have a gun.'

'Yeah, I thought of that.' This was easier, because this was the truth. 'Trouble is, I could only get a couple of them before—'

'If you're not a good shot,' she said quickly, 'I am.'

'That's not the problem.'

'Then what is?'

'We don't know how many headhunters there are, but we're certainly outnumbered. And our visitors will be bristling with poisoned darts, bows and arrows—against

our one gun.' Slade tried to smile. 'The odds aren't in
our favor.'

Brionny knew he was right.

'Then what do you suggest?'

Slade hesitated. 'There's one thing that might work.'

'What is it?'

'You're not going to like it.'

She smiled a little. 'I don't like the idea of being
turned into a Mali-Mali pincushion either. Try me.'

He drew a breath. 'If you give up the stone, we might
just have a chance.'

She didn't like it. The doubt came back into her eyes
and she shook her head, an automatic denial on her lips.

'I don't—'

That was as far as she got. A sound interrupted her,
carried toward them on the still morning air, a soft rus-
tling, as if an animal—or a man—was moving stealthily
through the trees.

Slade's heart slammed against his ribs. 'Shh,' he murmured.

Brionny sank back into his arms, her eyes fixed on
the tangle of greenery at the far side of the clearing.

Was someone coming? The leaves and vines were so
thick, the sun so faint as it tried to penetrate them, that
it was almost impossible to see anything, but she
thought—she thought she could see—

She managed only one swift intake of breath before
Slade's hand clapped over her mouth.

Below, branches and leaves shifted delicately, expos-
ing bits and pieces of the face that hid within them.
Brionny had a glimpse of dark eyes set in a broad
face—and then it was gone.

She swung toward Slade, her mouth trembling. He
nodded grimly and put his finger to his lips.

The time for negotiation was over.

Quickly he grabbed the backpack, jumped noiselessly to the ground, and held up his arms. Unhesitatingly Brionny dropped into them. He wanted to hold her close, ease the fear from her eyes, but there wasn't time.

'We'll be fine,' he whispered, wishing he really believed it. He kissed her gently before setting her on her feet. 'I won't let anything happen to you, sweetheart. I promise.'

He took her hand, the clasp of his fingers firm and comforting, and drew her swiftly into the trees.

CHAPTER SEVEN

THEY HAD been traveling through the rainforest for hours before Slade held up his hand.

'If you hear the Mali-Mali,' Brionny panted, 'I don't want to know about it.'

'Stuart—I think I know where we are!'

She would have laughed, but she didn't have the energy. 'So do I. We're smack in the middle of a big blank space on the map.'

'I read something about a mining company that came in here a few years ago.'

'So?'

'So, our luck may be improving.'

This time she did laugh. 'From what, McClintoch? Desperate to just plain awful?'

Slade pushed a tendril of damp hair back from her smudged face. 'Can you hang in a little longer?'

As if there were a choice, she thought. 'Sure,' she said, and followed after him, deeper into the jungle.

Miles later, she came staggering around a bend and stumbled into him.

'Slade,' she moaned, 'I can't go another step. Don't you think the Mali-Mali must have given up by now? If they were still after us, they'd have—'

'Listen!'

'Listen to what? I don't...' Brionny frowned. 'What is that?'

'Water,' Slade said, grinning like a schoolboy. 'Running water. If I'm right, it's a branch of the river.'

'Here?' It was too much to hope for. 'But—but it can't be.'

'That mining report mentioned a tributary that's supposed to cut through the forest somewhere in this vicinity.' Slade took her hand and they moved forward. 'It's not on the map so I wouldn't have wasted time searching for it, but going this distance cross-country may have put us right in line for—'

'Oh, Slade—look!' Ahead, a brown stream arrowed between sloping banks of dense vegetation. And tucked snugly against the nearest bank was a small, tin-roofed structure. 'A house!' Laughter bubbled from Brionny's throat. She turned and went spinning into Slade's arms. 'That means people, and a radio, and a boat—'

He shook his head. 'Don't expect miracles, sweetheart. It's probably just an old supply shed.'

Her face fell a little, but she kept smiling. 'It's still a miracle. The river, and a roof over our heads for the night—we can stay the night, can't we?'

He hadn't planned on it. Sunset was still hours away. If he worked fast, there was time to cut down some saplings, lash them together to form a raft—but how much further could he push Brionny? She'd already shown more courage and stamina than any woman he'd ever known.

She was probably right. If the Mali-Mali hadn't caught up to them by now, surely it meant they'd given up.

He smiled. 'OK. We'll get a good night's rest. First thing tomorrow morning, we'll build ourselves a raft.'

'A raft.' She sighed happily. 'And then, Italpa.'

'Yeah. We're almost home free,' Slade said, with just

a shade more conviction than he felt. He put his hand
under her chin, dipped his head, and brushed his mouth
over hers. 'To success.'

Their eyes met, and something deep inside his gut
knotted. Slowly, he bent to her again, giving her time
to make the choice—and she did. Brionny gave a little
sigh, tilted her head back, and offered him her lips.

How could she deny this moment? she thought as
Slade's head dropped to hers. They had teetered on the
brink of incredible disaster and come through un-
scathed. Surely a gentle, brief kiss to celebrate their
victory over the headhunters wasn't dangerous...?

It was like touching flame to dry kindling. Slade
groaned as their lips met—or was it she who made that
soft, impassioned sound? It didn't matter. Her arms
wound tightly around his neck as he gathered her to
him, his mouth opening in demand over hers. His hands
slid down her spine, cupped her buttocks, and lifted her
into the hard heat of his body.

Sensation swept through her in a dizzying rush.
'Slade?' she whispered.

'Yes, sweetheart.' He took one of her hands, kissed
it, then brought it between them. He placed it against
his chest and she felt the thudding beat of his heart.
'Tell me what you want.'

The question was simple, but the answer was complex. What did she want? Every time Slade touched her
she was swept away on an emotional roller coaster, and
she was never sure how she would feel at the end of
the ride.

Brionny's head drooped. 'I don't know,' she said
honestly. 'I'm too tired to think.'

Slade nodded. He had hoped for a different answer,
but she was right. This was no time to think of anything

but survival. He took a breath and clasped her shoulders gently.

'Well, I know what I want,' he said, smiling. 'A bath in that river, another gourmet dinner of dried fruit and nuts, and the chance to curl up on the floor in that elegant shack and sleep for the next twelve hours straight. How does that sound?'

Brionny's face lit. 'It sounds like heaven.'

Hand in hand, they made their way to the shack. Slade motioned her behind him as he slowly pushed open the door. It was dirty, hot and musty—but it was safe.

'Welcome to the local branch of the Hotel Florinda,' he said, with a grin.

Brionny shuddered as she stepped inside. 'The Florinda's a four-star establishment compared to this.'

'Come on, Stuart, where's your spirit of adventure? We've got four walls, a roof, a cot bed—' He dropped the pack to the floor and walked slowly across the room. 'Some kind soul's even left us a couple of tins of food.'

With a weary groan, Brionny sank down on the edge of the cot. 'Tinned ptomaine,' she sighed.

Slade chuckled. 'What you need is a nap. Tell you what. I'll scout around outside while you curl up here for a little while. How does that sound?'

'No.' She started to struggle to her feet. 'No, if you're not going to rest yet, I'll—'

Gently, he pressed her back down on the cot. 'It doesn't take two people to check the area,' he said. 'I only want to see if whoever built this place left behind anything else we might be able to use. OK?'

Brionny fell back on the cot. 'OK. You do that, and I'll see what I can do to make this place a little more liveable.'

He smiled. Her eyes were already closing. 'Good idea,' he whispered. He waited until her lashes lay against her cheeks, and then he went out the door.

She came awake in a rush, heart pounding. 'Slade?'

Silence greeted her. The shack was still and hot. Brionny frowned, sat up, and thrust her hands into her hair. How long had she been sleeping? Five minutes? An hour? Her watch had stopped working during their flight through the jungle; she had no idea what time it was or how much had passed.

She rose stiffly to her feet. Every muscle ached, and she groaned softly. Where was Slade anyway? He'd said he'd be just outside, but she couldn't hear anything out there except for the omnipresent chirp of insects.

Maybe insects were the only things out there. Maybe Slade was gone. Maybe something had happened to him. The headhunters might have come creeping out of the jungle, or—

She swung toward the door as it flew open. Slade stepped into the room.

'Hi,' he said. 'How are you feeling?'

Her breath caught. He was shirtless and shoeless, dressed only in his jeans, and they were soaking wet, clinging to his long, muscular legs and narrow hips like a second skin.

He'd been swimming, she thought dizzily. Water gleamed in his dark hair, droplets of it dappling his golden shoulders and glinting in the swirls of hair that covered his chest.

Brionny's throat constricted. How beautifully male he was, how perfect. Her gaze drifted down his torso, taking in the well-defined muscles, the hard belly. A dark arrow of hair led down to his jeans, dipped under the opened waistband, disappeared behind the taut, wet denim...

Heat shot through her, piercing her breast and pooling deep in her loins.

'Bree?'

Her eyes shot to his. His smile had faded; he was watching her with the intensity of a jaguar stalking its prey.

'Bree,' he said again, his voice a husky whisper, and he started toward her.

She shook her head and took a step back. 'Slade, don't.'

'Bree, sweetheart.' He reached out for her, his hands hard but his smile persuasive. 'Why should we go on playing this game?' Her eyes closed as he brushed soft kisses along her face. 'We both know what's been happening. We've known since the day we met at the Florinda...'

His arms were tightening around her. He kissed her, his mouth hot, his tongue insistent. She was melting, she thought desperately, melting in his heat...

But she had melted before, in the arms of a man like this one, a man who'd also known just the right words to whisper, just the right places to touch and kiss...

She tore her mouth from Slade's.

'Stop it,' she said sharply.

His head lifted. His eyes were dark and puzzled. 'Bree?'

'Don't "Bree" me,' she snapped, and wrenched free of his embrace. 'I swear, if you touch me again—'

'If *I* touch *you* again?' Color flared across his high cheekbones. 'Who are you kidding? You were all over me, lady, with about as much subtlety as a cat in heat!'

Her hand shot through the air and exploded against

his cheek. He caught her wrist and dragged it behind her back.

'I warned you before about this little game you play, Stuart. How many times do you think you can turn a man on and off before you get in over your head?'

'Listen, McClintoch, when we reach Italpa—'

Slade smiled tightly. 'Don't you mean *if*?'

'When we do,' Brionny said with cold determination, 'you're going to get what's coming to you.'

He laughed. 'I already have. These couple of days in your company have been like a lifetime sentence in hell. The Mali-Mali don't know how lucky they were, being denied the pleasure of your gracious presence, Stuart.'

Brionny yanked the door open and marched outside. 'Why don't you open one of those tins and have something to eat?' she said, flinging the words over her shoulder. 'With luck, you'll get food poisoning.'

'Stuart.' Slade's voice called after her. 'Stuart! Where do you think you're going?'

She turned and looked at him, her smile as cold and unforgiving as her eyes.

'For a swim, McClintoch. Any objections?'

He glared at her. 'Just don't take too long.'

'Why?' she said sweetly. 'Are you afraid I'll use up all the warm water in these magnificent accommodations you found us?'

'I was thinking of the possibility of intruders, Stuart. Caimans or piranhas or such.' He folded his arms across his naked chest. 'Snakes, too, but hell, what is there to worry about? There's nothing out there with fangs sharper than yours.'

Brionny's chin lifted. 'Just remember that,' she said.

She turned, kicked off her boots and, still dressed, dove into the water.

It was warm, almost unpleasantly so, but at least it would wash away the dirt and sweat.

Damn Slade McClintoch, she thought furiously. The man was impossible. The sooner they parted company the better.

She ducked under the water and came up, tossing her wet hair back from her face.

How dared he accuse her of playing games? She wasn't the one. It was he who—

Something bumped gently against her calf. She held her breath and looked around her. There was nothing to see except some branches, carried by the current. That was what she'd felt—a branch or—

Something bumped her leg again. And again. And—

A long, sinuous body, as thick around as a man's thigh or the trunk of a tree, broke the surface of the water beside her. For an instant Brionny stared at the huge snake, enraptured by its cold beauty, and then a scream burst from her throat.

Slade called her name. She heard him dive into the water.

'Get to shore,' he shouted, and she obeyed blindly, falling to her knees among the reeds.

She scrambled to her feet and stared out at the river. The water was churning, turned to foam by Slade and the snake. It was impossible to see anything clearly...

Everything went still. There was nothing visible, not the snake—not Slade. Brionny began to tremble.

'No,' she said. Her voice rose in panic. 'Slade, no—'

He rose from the water, gasping for breath. Brionny flew to him as he stumbled to shore and threw her arms around him.

'Slade,' she sobbed, 'I thought the snake had—'

'You damned fool!' He caught her by the shoulders and shook her, his eyes blazing with fury. 'You could have been killed!'

'I only went for a swim,' she said in a choked voice. 'You said—you said it was safe.'

'The hell I did!'

'Don't yell at me,' she said—and, to her horror, she burst into tears.

Slade glared at her. 'Stop it,' he growled. 'Dammit, Stuart, did you hear me? I told you to— Oh, hell.' His arms swept around her and he held her to him so tightly that she could feel the thudding beat of his heart. 'Bree, sweetheart, don't cry.'

But she couldn't seem to stop. The weariness and terror of the past days had finally overcome her; she buried her face in his shoulder and wept and wept, her arms looped around his waist.

Slade pressed his lips to her hair. 'It's OK, sweetheart. It's all over now.'

'I'm sorry,' she said brokenly. 'I've been nothing but trouble, and I know it.'

'Shh.' Slade swept her into his arms and carried her into the shack. He sat down with her in his lap on the cot. 'Shh,' he said again, rocking her gently. She gave a little sigh and wiped her nose, and he smiled. 'Better?'

'Yes.' She hesitated. 'I never saw that horrible thing until—'

'Hush, sweetheart. I should have stopped you from going into the water but I was so—so—'

'Angry, I know.'

'Not angry.' His arms tightened around her. 'I saw the way you looked at me when I came through that doorway. I knew what you were feeling, how your heart was racing—'

Her cheeks turned pink with embarrassment. 'I don't want to talk about it.'

'And then I saw you regret those feelings. I saw you judge me—and find me wanting.'

'It—it isn't that simple, Slade. I know you think it is, but—'

'Hell, I don't think it's simple at all. It's what happens to me whenever I look at you.' He made a sound that was not quite a laugh. 'I'm never sure if I want to turn you over my knee and paddle you or take you into my arms and make love to you until neither of us has the strength to move.'

Color flew into her face. 'Is—is that really how I make you feel?' she whispered.

Slade groaned softly. 'Here's how you make me feel,' he said, and kissed her.

Brionny held still for an instant, and then she sighed, wound her arms around his neck, and kissed him back.

It was Slade who ended the kiss. 'This situation's a mess,' he said, 'and I'm to blame. I've been so stupid and stubborn—'

'Not you. Me.' She laid her palm against his cheek, loving the feel of his beard-roughened skin. 'You've saved my life more times than I can count, and, instead of being grateful, I pay you back with—'

'Dammit, I don't want your gratitude!' Slade tumbled her back on the mattress and glared down at her. 'Brionny, we have to talk.'

'Yes. I suppose we do.' She gave a muffled yawn. 'Sorry. I'd forgotten how nice a real bed feels.'

He couldn't help grinning. 'Hey, Stuart, you already had half an hour's sack time. It's my turn, remember?'

She smiled and held up her arms. 'How about if we share?' she said softly.

'Bree, please. Just stay awake for another few minutes. There's so much I need to tell you—'

Brionny looped her arms around Slade's neck. 'Can't it wait a little while longer?' she whispered sleepily.

With a muffled groan, he came down beside her and gathered her into his arms. The truth about himself had already waited this long, he thought; what did another few hours matter?

'Why not?' he said.

Slade's eyes closed, as did Brionny's. Within seconds, they were asleep.

Brionny awoke to heat, blazing heat that encompassed her.

Her eyes opened slowly; it took a moment to orient herself. The shack, she thought, that was where she was—with Slade.

Slade. Brionny's breathing quickened. It was his heat she felt. Some time during the hours they'd been sleeping, she had turned on to her back while he had rolled on to his belly. Now they were lying entangled, his leg across hers, his arm draped over her in a gesture that was as possessive as it was protective. His hand was lightly curved over her breast. She felt her nipples harden, felt an answering constriction deep in her womb. She swallowed and shut her eyes. It was only a physiological reaction. She had done enough experiments to know that you couldn't control nerve and muscle responses.

Slade murmured in his sleep, rolled on to his side. His hand moved against her breast, his fingers brushing lightly over her swollen flesh. She bit back a soft whimper. Just a physiological reaction, she told herself desperately, that was all it was…

'Brionny. I thought you were a dream.'

Slade's voice was low. It sent a tremor of longing down her spine.

'Slade. I—I didn't mean to wake you.'

'I felt the heat of your skin, smelled its perfume.' He moved a little, rose up so that he was looking down into her face. 'I felt the softness of you here, under my fingertips—'

'Slade—it must be late. Shouldn't we—shouldn't we—?'

'Bree.' He took his hand from her breast, curved it under her chin. 'I want to make love to you.'

She looked up at him, at the eyes she had once thought cold, the mouth she'd thought insolent. He lowered his head slowly and kissed her, his lips catching at hers, shaping them to his desire.

Brionny stirred beneath the kiss, and her breathing quickened.

Slade drew back. 'Tell me you want me too, Brionny.'

Maybe it was the darkness, lightened only by the moonglow streaming through the window. Maybe it was the sensation of being suspended in time and space. Whatever it was, Brionny knew that the time for denial was over.

With a little cry, she reached for Slade and brought his mouth to hers.

His kisses were gentle at first, soft touches that were like the brush of butterfly wings, but as she began to return them they deepened, grew more intense. His tongue slipped between her lips, slid along the soft inner lining of her mouth.

Brionny made a soft, urgent sound in the back of her throat and ran her hands up Slade's naked chest, exploring the soft mat of dark hair that covered it, skimming over the taut pectoral muscles, the flat washboard abdominals.

Slade groaned, caught her hand, brought it to his lips and pressed his open mouth to her palm.

'Do you have any idea how much I want you?' he whispered.

She smiled. 'Tell me.'

He did, but not with words. He showed her by kissing her deeply, his tongue moving against hers in long, hot strokes. He kissed her at the soft place just behind her ear. When she shivered, he smiled against her skin, then trailed his lips the length of her throat.

He drew back a little, stroked his hand lightly over her cotton shirt, shaping her breast, cupping it, and then he dipped his head and took the fabric-covered nipple gently between his teeth.

Brionny cried out and arched against him.

'Slowly,' he whispered, 'slowly, love. There's no rush.'

He drew her flesh into the damp warmth of his mouth, teasing her with soft kisses and softer bites until she was moving blindly against him, and then he sat her up and slipped the shirt over her head.

'Beautiful,' he said, cupping her breasts in his hands. His thumbs moved gently against her nipples. 'I've never forgotten seeing you in that pool,' he whispered, 'the soft ivory and pink of your breasts. I wondered if they would taste as sweet and silken as they looked.'

She trembled as he traced the fullness of her flesh, first with his hands, then with his lips. He rubbed his cheek against the tender skin. It was days since he'd shaved; his beard was soft, feathery light, its touch so electrifying that she cried out. He touched his tongue to one rosy crest and she held her breath, waiting for the moment when he would take a deeper, hungrier taste. When he did, when his teeth closed lightly on the puckered bud, flame shot through Brionny's body and pooled like liquid fire between her thighs.

'Sweeter,' he whispered, 'sweeter than honey.'

He moved up over her, kissing her mouth while his hand slipped over her belly. He undid the button at her waistband and she whimpered as his fingers slid inside her shorts. His hand moved down and down, and finally his thumb stroked across her, sliding with agonizing slowness against her nylon-covered flesh, and she arched against his finger and cried out his name.

'Do you want me to touch you?' he whispered. 'Tell me what you want.'

Were the words an echo of some darker time? It was too late to wonder or to think. Brionny whispered her answer in shameless abandon, lifting her hips so that Slade could ease away the rest of her clothing.

Then he drew back. She watched as his hands went to his jeans. Slowly, he slid them from his body.

He was perfect, as she had known he would be. The broad shoulders and muscled chest tapered to a narrow waist and hips. His legs were long and muscular—and his sex was proud and exciting, rising from the dark, lush hair that surrounded it.

'You're beautiful,' she whispered, and he smiled. He ran his hands over her again, as if to memorize every soft curve. Gently, he parted her thighs. He kissed the softness of her skin, breathed in her scent, buried his face against her and kissed her intimately until she cried out. Then he lifted his head, looked at her face, watched her as he slid his fingers against her slick, wet flesh.

Brionny arched toward him in ecstasy. She reached

for him, needing to touch him as he was touching her. Her fingers curled around him, as far as they could. He was hot, like flame, as hard as steel yet with the smoothness of silk, and she stroked him, her rhythm matching his until, with a startled cry, she exploded against his hand.

Slade growled his triumph. He bent and kissed her, taking her soft moans into his mouth, and then he drew back.

'Bree,' he whispered.

Her lashes fluttered open. She looked at him, at his dangerous smile, at the dark green fire of his eyes. Slowly he leaned forward, not to enter her but to brush the fullness of his sex against her swollen flesh. Sensation shot through her again, arrowing from her dewy center to every part of her body, and she knew that what had just happened was only the beginning.

'I want to see your eyes as you take me inside you.'

'Slade,' she sobbed, 'Slade, please—'

But he was relentless, moving himself back and forth against her until she was mindless with abandon. Then, at last, he entered her.

Brionny clasped his head, dragged his mouth down to hers. Slade was filling her beyond anything she had ever imagined, not just physically but in a million other ways.

She cried out as he began to move, pulling back slowly then rocking forward, his hands beneath her, cupping her buttocks, lifting her to him. He caught her mouth with his, his tongue duplicating the motions of his body. Suddenly she tensed, dazzled with pleasure yet terrified, knowing he wanted to take her to a place so high that she might reach it and tumble off into space.

'Come with me,' he whispered. 'Come with me, love, come—'

There was no way to resist. Sobbing his name, Brionny gave herself up to him, riding his passion and making it hers. She shattered in his arms, bursting into a million pieces as bright as sunlight, soaring up and up into the sky. Then, slowly, she drifted to earth again, safe in Slade's embrace.

He kissed her throat, nipped lightly at her skin, and began to roll away, but she held him close, loving the weight of his body on hers. She wanted to feel the slowing beat of his heart, the silken dampness of his skin.

'You're wonderful,' he whispered.

She smiled as she stroked her fingers through his hair. 'It wasn't me,' she said, 'it was—' It was because I love you, she'd almost said.

The thought stunned her. Did she love him? Was that why what she'd felt in his arms just now had been so incredible?

She was willing to admit she'd misjudged him. He might be an adventurer, a man who chased dreams, but he certainly wasn't evil, he wasn't—

'It was what?' he said.

Brionny sighed. 'It was you,' she murmured, unwilling to give voice just yet to that last, confusing thought.

Slade kissed her and rolled on to his side, still holding her close.

'Shut your eyes, sweetheart, and sleep. We'll need all the rest we can get before morning.'

Brionny's smile dimmed. For just a little while, she'd forgotten their situation.

'Slade? Do you really think we've lost the Mali-Mali?'

Maybe, he thought.

'I hope so,' he said.

'What—what if we haven't? What if they come after us again?'

It was a good question, and it needed a good answer.

'Then I'll do everything in my power to protect you,' he said.

He kissed her, then drew her head into the crook of his shoulder. Brionny snuggled against him. She was almost asleep when Slade whispered her name.

'Bree?'

'Mmm?'

'You never did tell me where you hid the Eye of God.'

She hesitated. She knew what he was asking. Do you trust me now? he was saying. Do you trust me with your secret, now that you've trusted me with your body?

She took a deep, deep breath. 'It's in the box of tampons. I didn't think you'd look there.'

He smiled, and then he laughed softly. 'No. It's the one place I'd never have checked.' His arms tightened around her. 'Go to sleep now, sweetheart.'

It took a while. She felt strangely uneasy. But, eventually, she did.

She dreamed she was entering a great hall, one that looked like the museum's but was a hundred times bigger. People were rising to their feet and applauding— the Mayor, the director, the members of the board—but she brushed past them, looking for just one face.

'Señorita?'

She was mounting the steps to the podium now, where the Eye of God waited, glowing like emerald fire.

'Señorita. Habla usted español?'

The audience was waiting for her to speak but she couldn't, not until she found Slade.

But it wasn't Slade she saw as she came abruptly awake. There was a stranger standing over her, a tall, cadaverous-looking man in a black suit. Heart racing, she clutched the tattered blanket to her throat and sat up.

'Wh-who are you?' she stammered. 'What do you want?'

The man raised his hands, as if in benediction. 'Do not be afraid, *señorita*. I am Father Ramón, of the Mission of San Luis.'

'The mission of…?' She could see his clerical collar now, and the cross swinging from his neck. Brionny blew out her breath. 'You scared the life out of me, Father.'

'That was surely not my intention,' he said solemnly.

'But-where did you come from?'

'Our mission is just upriver, *señorita*. Some of my flock were out hunting. They stopped here, as they have done before, and found something most unexpected.' Father Ramón came closer, his eyes politely fixed on a point just beyond Brionny's shoulder. 'How have you come to be here, *señorita?*'

'It's a long story, Father, and we'll be happy to tell it to you as soon as—'

'We, *señorita?*'

'Could you just turn your back for a minute, Father? I'd like to-to dress before—'

The missionary turned away. 'Of course. Forgive me for intruding upon you, but when my people said there was a *gringa* here—'

'Don't apologize, please.' Brionny dressed quickly, ran her hands through her hair, and cleared her throat. 'You can turn around now.'

'We thought you might be ill,' he said as he swung toward her.

'No, no, I'm fine.' She peered past him, trying to see outside. 'Didn't Slade answer any of your questions?'

'Who?'

'The man—' She felt her cheeks pinken. 'The man I'm traveling with. We had no idea we were so close to civilization, and... Where is he, anyway? Oh, he must have been so pleased to see you!'

'There is no one here but you, *señorita.*'

'Don't be silly.' Brionny brushed past Father Ramón and stepped into the sunlight. An handful of Indians dressed in Western clothes stared at her. 'Slade?' She frowned as she turned in a little circle. 'Slade, where are you?'

'*Señorita,*' the missionary said firmly, 'you are alone here.' He hesitated. 'Perhaps you *have* been ill. There are some jungle fevers that cause hallucinations and—'

'The Mali-Mali! They must have taken him!'

'The headhunters?' Her made the sign of the cross. 'They have not raided for years, thanks be to God.'

Brionny turned toward him, her face flushed. 'I'm telling you, they've taken Slade! Your men must go after them!'

'*Señorita,* calm yourself. Had the savages been here, they would have left signs to inspire fear in others. It is their custom.'

'To hell with their custom! If Slade's gone, it's because they took him!'

'Blasphemy will not help, *señorita.*'

'Neither will sanctimony! I saw them, I tell you.'

'What did you see, *señorita?*'

'Indians. Well, an Indian, but—'

'Why would you not see an Indian?' the priest asked with a little smile. 'There are many of them who live here, in the Amazon.'

'Father, please. While you stand around insisting nothing's happened to Slade, the Mali-Mali could be—'

'*If* there had been a man with you, and *if* the savages had taken him, do you think it likely they would have left you behind?'

Brionny's mouth opened, then closed. There was logic in his argument. But if Slade hadn't been taken away...

A coldness crept around her heart, squeezing it like an icy fist. She spun toward the door and flung it open.

Hours ago, a million years ago, Slade had undressed her and then himself. He'd flung his clothing into the corner.

Now that corner was empty. Slade's shirt, his jeans, his shoes—everything was gone. All that remained was her gun and her backpack. It lay upended, the tampon box ripped open and the contents a spill of white across the dirt floor.

With a cry of despair, Brionny buried her face in hands,.

'You see?' she heard the missionary say gently. 'It is as I suspected. You are ill, *señorita.* Let me help you.'

But no one could help her, Brionny thought as Father Ramón led her from the shack.

Slade was gone, and so was the Eye of God.

CHAPTER EIGHT

BRIONNY SAT sat in her stuffy basement office, her fingers resting lightly on her computer keyboard, her eyes scanning the pages of her report as it flashed across the monitor.

...set within a niche on what had been an altar in the Forbidden City...
...smaller than the size we'd imagined but larger than...
...deep green in color, with no imperfections or striations visible to the naked eye...

The words blurred together. She muttered under her breath, hit a key, and the screen went blank.

The report was no good. She had an appointment with the museum director in less than an hour and what would she hand him? Surely not this piece of fluff.

She'd been writing the thing for days, and it still sounded more like a travelog than a scientific rendering of how she and Professor Ingram had found the Eye of God.

No. No, that wasn't really true. The report was perfectly fine—to a point. She'd had no trouble describing what had led up to their locating the emerald, nor had it been difficult to depict the stone.

The problem had started when she'd tried to explain what had happened to it after that.

'How could you, of all people, have been such a fool?' her father had said, when she'd told him what had happened—and she hadn't told him anything but the essentials: that she'd thrown in her lot with a stranger, and that he'd ultimately made off with the treasure she and Professor Ingram had found.

Her mother had hushed him, pointing out that Brionny's only choice had been to combine forces with the stranger, that she'd been left alone in the jungle and that there'd been headhunters pursuing her—

'You mean,' Henry Stuart had said, displeasure thinning his lips, 'she *thought* there were headhunters pursuing her.'

'That's enough, Henry,' Eve Stuart had said, her eyes snapping out a warning—but it really hadn't mattered.

Her father was right. The story about the Mali-Mali had been an outright lie, nothing but the cheapest fiction—and she'd fallen for it. She'd let Slade McClintoch spin a web of deceit that a child could have seen through. He had turned her to clay in his treacherous hands and then he had stripped her of her dignity as a scientist—and as a woman.

If only she could forget that long, humiliating night she'd spent in his arms, the things she'd done, the things she'd let him do…

Brionny shoved back her chair and jumped to her feet.

'Damn the heat in this place!'

She glared at the ancient air conditioner, chugging away uselessly in the wall, as if the machine were to blame for her mood. He couldn't fix it, the janitor had said when she'd complained; there was no money for buying new units for the basement.

And the basement, Brionny suspected, was where she and her career were going to stay—unless she lucked into a miracle.

Maybe she could force the window open. It was hot outside, but hot air that was fresh would be better than the recirculated stuff that was pumping through her office.

The window wouldn't budge. Layers of paint had mixed with years of soot to form an impenetrable bond. She gave the sash a last, angry thump with the heel of her hand.

'Damn,' she said. Her shoulders slumped. 'Oh, hell,' she muttered, and she gave a tired little laugh and plopped herself down on the wide sill.

Was this really what she'd been reduced to? Cursing windows and air conditioners and storming around her steamy cubicle of an office like a frustrated rat in a maze?

None of that would put her career back on track.

'What happened was not your fault,' her mother kept saying.

But it was.

She was already being talked of as the woman who'd let the Eye of God slip through her fingers.

Yesterday the girl in the next office—a graduate student in geology—had introduced Brionny to her boyfriend.

'This is Brionny Stuart,' she'd gushed, 'the-girl-who-lost-that-fabulous-emerald-in-the-Amazon.'

It had been said just that way, all in one breath, as if the designation were part of her name, as if she had no other identity and never would have.

Even that had been an act of kindness, because saying she'd 'lost' the stone was a polite euphemism for the truth, which was that she'd been stupid enough to let an opportunistic stranger steal it—and nobody even knew exactly how he'd managed that.

Not yet, anyway.

Brionny shuddered. Would she ever live down the disgrace? Maybe not, but she wouldn't go down without a fight. She'd take Slade with her, see to it that he was caught and tossed into prison for a long, long time.

'It's just too bad they don't guillotine people for what you did, McClintoch,' she muttered, her flushed face taking on a look of grim determination.

She'd tried taking the first step. She'd gone straight to the police after she'd finally reached Italpa in a dugout paddled by Father Ramón's Indians. Unfortunately, the lone policeman on duty had seemed more interested in admiring her legs than in taking notes—but surely things would get moving now.

This morning she was meeting with Simon Esterhaus, the director of the museum. He'd been away when she'd returned from the Amazon, so there'd been no one to take her official report, but he was back now, and, as his secretary had made clear, this meeting with Brionny was at the top of his agenda.

Brionny glanced at her watch, then rose from the sill and dusted off her skirt. Ten minutes to zero hour, she thought, and tried to calm her suddenly racing pulse.

'The director will expect you at ten-thirty,' Esterhaus's secretary had said crisply. 'He wishes to talk with you privately before his eleven o'clock appointment arrives.'

'Someone will be joining us, you mean?'

'That is correct, Miss Stuart. Please be prompt.'

The woman had broken the connection before
Brionny could ask any questions, but it hadn't really
been necessary. She could make a pretty good guess at
who the third party at the meeting would be. Esterhaus
had obviously contacted the authorities—the New York
police, perhaps, or a firm of private investigators.
They'd expect her to tell them everything.

Her stomach clenched as she closed her office door
behind her. She would do that, she thought, her heels
clicking sharply against the tile as she made her way to
the stairs to the Great Hall. She would tell them everything—everything but the final, ugly truth: that she'd
gone willingly into Slade's arms, that he'd made love
to her, that she'd told him—*told* him!—where she'd
hidden the Eye of God.

Brionny's face flamed scarlet.

There was no need for anyone to know those details.
No need at all.

'Be prompt', the secretary had warned, but Brionny was
kept cooling her heels in the waiting room for more than
half an hour.

An act of intimidation, she decided. Not that any was
necessary. She was nervous to begin with, and the director had a formidable reputation. The staff joked that
he had a calculator where he should have had a heart.

Now, as she finally entered his office, she saw that it
had all the trappings of power. The room was enormous,
its furnishings elegant. Choice relics from the museum's
vast collection adorned the walls and tables, and what
seemed like an acre of magnificent Persian carpet
stretched between the door and his Queen Anne desk.

Esterhaus smiled politely.

'Come in, Miss Stuart.' He waved a bony hand to a

chair opposite his desk. 'Sorry to have kept you waiting.' He tilted back his chair and steepled his fingers beneath his chin. 'Well, let's get right to it, shall we? I know the basics of what happened in Peru. What I need now are the details.'

Brionny nodded. 'Yes, sir.'

'How unfortunate, my dear, that your very first expedition for us should have ended so badly for you.'

A good shot, Brionny thought. In one sentence Esterhaus had established both her guilt and the tenuousness of her position.

'I myself have never had the pleasure of going into the field.' He smiled, showing feral white teeth. 'But then, my area of expertise is so dull compared to the exotic nature of yours.'

Shot two, and straight across the bow. Esterhaus had neatly pointed out that it was administrators such as he who kept scientists such as she in business.

Cut to the chase, Brionny told herself. She cleared her throat and shifted forward in the chair.

'Mr Esterhaus, I know how distressed you must be at the loss of the Eye of God. Exhibiting it would have brought us great prestige.'

'You are direct, Miss Stuart. I admire that. Yes, you're quite right. An exhibit of the emerald would have brought us prestige, and a lot of money—surely enough to have justified the cost of the expedition.' Esterhaus's chair tilted forward, and he tapped a finger against a stack of papers on his desk. 'Professor Ingram was so sure he would be bringing the stone back that I'd indulged myself in a little judicious daydreaming.' His teeth glinted again in a rapacious smile. 'You'd be amazed at the admission fees the public's willing to pay to see something so ancient.'

'Sir, no one is sorrier than I for what happened, but—'

'What *did* happen, pray tell? As you said a moment ago, you lost the stone.' Esterhaus smiled again, but his eyes were flat and cold behind his spectacles. 'Such a quaint way of putting it, don't you think? One may lose a pen, or a wallet, but losing a priceless relic—well, it's not quite the same thing, is it?'

'I assure you, Mr Esterhaus, I safeguarded the stone as best I could, but circumstance—'

'Your rescuer, that missionary—what was his name?'

'Father Ramón.'

'Father Ramón. Yes. I'm afraid the message he sent us was not terribly clear.' Esterhaus moistened the tip of his index finger and began shuffling through his papers. 'I have a transcript of it here somewhere...' He looked up, frowning. 'I'm sure you know what he said, Miss Stuart. Ramón thought you might have been delirious. He said you were raving about headhunters, and about a man who was supposedly with you.'

Brionny swallowed. 'I wasn't delirious. I—I'd had reason to believe there were headhunters after us, and—and there was a man with me.'

Esterhaus's brows arched. 'Indeed?'

She hesitated, wondering if Esterhaus could hear the pounding of her heart. 'He was the one who—who stole the emerald from me.'

The director took off his rimless eyeglasses, held them to the light, then popped them back on his nose.

'I must say, Miss Stuart, I'm delighted you've decided to be up front about this.'

'Sir?'

'Taking up with a strange man, letting him get a priceless relic in his hands—those were very poor decisions to have made. I admire your honesty in admitting your errors.'

His tone, and his smile, made it clear that the only thing he admired was the swiftness with which they'd come to what had to be the heart of the interview.

'That isn't exactly accurate, sir. I didn't "take up" with this man. Professor Ingram was dead, my guides had abandoned me, and a tribe of headhunters was—'

'There was never any danger from headhunters. Father Ramón's message makes it clear that he explained that to you.'

'I know that now, Mr Esterhaus. But at the time I thought—'

'How did this man take the stone from you, Miss Stuart?'

'He—he just did.'

'By force?'

Brionny flushed. 'No. Not—not by force.'

'By intimidation?'

'No, sir. He—uh—he simply found it, and—'

'Found it? You mean you'd hidden it?'

'Yes.'

'But not terribly well, hmm?' Esterhaus pursed his lips. 'When he took the stone, did you try to stop him?'

'I couldn't. He took it during the night, sir. I was asleep, and—and…' Her throat constricted. 'I did what I could, Mr Esterhaus. I reported the theft to the police in Italpa—'

'The police in Italpa,' Esterhaus said with a little laugh. 'A waste of time, Miss Stuart. A joke! I've no intention of involving them in such serious business.'

Brionny nodded. 'I can understand that, sir, but I did try to—'

'It would be appropriate for me to ask for your resignation at this moment. You know that, of course.'

'Mr Esterhaus,' she said, fighting to keep her voice neutral, 'I know I made some errors in judgement, but I promise I'll do whatever I possibly can to—'

The shrill of Esterhaus's telephone silenced her. She waited while he took the call.

'Good,' he said, 'very good. Ask him to wait just a moment, please.' He smiled as he hung up the phone. 'Did my secretary tell you about the gentleman who'll be joining us this morning?'

'No, not really. She only mentioned that someone would be—'

'Unfortunately he was unavoidably delayed, which means I'll have to curtail my plans to meet with the two of you together.' Esterhaus shot back his cuff, looked at his watch, and frowned importantly. 'I have a luncheon appointment with the Mayor,' he said, and smiled. 'But you'll be able to manage without me, I'm sure.'

'Yes, sir.'

'He'll need to know everything you can tell him about your unfortunate experience in the Amazon, Miss Stuart. Do you understand?'

Brionny flushed. Not everything, she thought. 'I'll—I'll do my best,' she said.

'It's vital that you do. With sufficient information, I have reason to believe we have a good chance of recovering the emerald.'

'That's wonderful!' Brionny's face lit with excitement. 'I'd like nothing better than to see the man who stole it caught and—'

'Your personal need for vengeance is not the museum's concern,' Esterhaus said coldly. 'Recovering the stone is our sole interest.'

'But it's the same thing, isn't it? Catching the thief and getting back the Eye—'

'Think, Miss Stuart, think! There are circumstances in which the one might cancel out the other.'

'I don't understand, Mr Esterhaus.'

The director sighed. 'If we can take the thief to trial, we will. But if we have no choice but to buy the stone back—'

'Buy it back?' she said, her voice rising.

'It is entirely possible we may have to negotiate for the emerald's return.'

'But—that's blackmail. It's ransom. It's—'

'It's business,' the director said sharply, 'and it's done all the time.'

Brionny wanted to tell him he was wrong—but she couldn't. Occasional whispers surfaced about a museum or gallery recovering a stolen object by 'buying it back' from the thieves who'd stolen it. The excuse was always the same—that the principals involved hadn't realized they'd been dealing with crooks—but no one really believed that.

'Even if you wanted to make such a deal,' she said slowly, 'how do you know the emerald hasn't already been sold on the black market?'

'I have it on good authority that the thief is lying low with the stone.' Esterhaus stood up and came around the desk. 'You see,' he said as Brionny got to her feet, 'we've had the most incredible good luck.' Smiling, he clasped her elbow in his skeletal hand. 'The gentleman you're about to meet contacted me several days ago.'

'While you were away?' Brionny threw him a bewildered look as he led her toward the door.

Esterhaus nodded. 'He was in Peru when the emerald disappeared.' They had reached the door, and he let go of Brionny's arm and put his hand on the knob. 'He's privy to some inside information.'

Brionny's heart thumped. 'Can he lead us to the thief?'

'He believes he can, and that's where you come in. He'll need you to help him identify the man—and the stone, too.'

A chill as cold as the grave whisked across the nape of Brionny's neck. It made no sense, but she could feel the hair rising on her skin.

'Therefore, Miss Stuart, as of this date, you are relieved of your duties at the museum.'

She paled. 'You're dismissing me? But I thought you said—'

'I am reassigning you. You will devote yourself to helping find the thief and the emerald. When the stone is safely in my hands, I shall wipe the slate clean and see to it that you are awarded your doctorate.' The director smiled benevolently. 'How does that sound, my dear?'

It sounded like the best news she'd had in weeks. So why was that chill dancing across her skin again?

'Sir,' she said quickly, 'wait a minute. Who is this man you—?'

Esterhaus flung the door open. Framed in it was his secretary's desk. The woman's flushed face was tilted up to an unseen figure standing beside her.

'Oh, go on,' she said, giggling happily, 'you don't really mean...'

Esterhaus cleared his throat. His secretary gave a startled jump.

'Mr Esterhaus. I didn't hear you, sir.'

Esterhaus took Brionny's arm and drew her forward. 'Miss Stuart,' he said, 'I'd like you to meet—'

But Brionny knew. She knew even before the man turned toward her.

It was Slade.

He had traded his jeans for a perfectly tailored gray suit, but everything else about him was the same, from that whipcord-hard body to the cool, emerald-green eyes.

Brionny made a choked sound. Esterhaus frowned.

'Miss Stuart?'

Slade laughed politely. 'I don't think I mentioned it, Esterhaus, but Miss Stuart and I have met before.'

'I don't believe it,' Brionny whispered.

Slade's eyes, cold with derision and warning, met hers.

'Surprise,' he said softly.

She spun toward Esterhaus, whose expression was puzzled. 'I didn't realize you two knew each other,' he said.

'Knew each other?' Brionny gave a cackling laugh. '*Knew* each other? Mr Esterhaus, this man—'

'Certainly we know each other.' Slade's voice was silky. He reached out, took Brionny's limp hand, and clasped it in his. It seemed a simple, friendly gesture; only she could feel the almost painful pressure he was exerting. 'Miss Stuart and I met in Italpa. We were guests at the same hotel and—' he shot Esterhaus a knowing, man-to-man smile '—we ran into some— ah—some personal problems, I'm afraid.'

'We didn't,' Brionny said desperately, 'We never had any personal prob—'

'I think she might still be annoyed with me, Simon, if you get my meaning.'

Simon? *Simon?* Brionny tried to wrench her hand from Slade's, but his callused fingers gripped hers like steel.

'Mr Esterhaus,' she said desperately, 'you've made a terrible mistake. You said the museum had been contacted by a gentleman, but you were wrong! Slade McClintoch is—'

'Now, now, Bree.' Slade chuckled as he stepped to her side and slipped his arm around her shoulders. His fingers bit into her flesh. 'We don't want to wash our dirty linen in public, do we, sweetheart?'

'Mr Esterhaus, dammit, this man—'

'That is enough, Miss Stuart.' Esterhaus's eyes were like chips of ice in his bony face. 'Whatever happened between you and Mr McClintoch in Italpa is your problem, not the museum's.' He looked at Slade and smiled. 'I look forward to swift and satisfactory progress.'

'Of course, Simon.'

Brionny made one last, futile effort. 'Wait,' she said.

The door to Esterhaus's office slammed in her face. With a little cry of fury and despair, she swung toward Slade. The polite smile he'd worn for the museum director was gone, replaced by a look of arrogance and utter contempt.

'You bastard,' she whispered, and he laughed coldly.

'I'm delighted to see you again too, sweetheart,' he said, and he put his hand in the small of her back and marched her past the desk of Esterhaus's goggle-eyed secretary, across the museum's Great Hall, and down the wide marble steps into the street.

CHAPTER NINE

THE INSTANT they reached the pavement, Brionny spun away from Slade and came to a stop. She was trembling with anger; her face was as pale as ivory, except for a flag of crimson high on each cheek.

'You fraud,' she said. 'You liar! You—you—'

'You really should try working up a new routine, Stuart. That litany's getting kind of dull.'

'You've got one minute to explain what you think you're doing, and then I'm going to march straight back to Esterhaus's office and blow your pathetic little cover story to smithereens.'

A smile tilted across Slade's mouth, although his eyes remained cold.

'Threats?' he said, his voice soft as silk.

'Promises, McClintoch.'

'You'll change your mind after we talk.'

'We have nothing to talk about.' Brionny put her hands on her hips. 'Unless you want to talk about your prison sentence.'

His mouth tightened into a hard line. 'This isn't the place for this discussion.'

'Ah. Where is the place, then? The local police station? The court house? Perhaps the director's office?'

Slade moved closer to her. There was a sense of tightly controlled anger about him, and it took all her concentration not to step back.

'Do you see that car at the curb?'

She looked past him. A bright red sports car was pulled up next to a 'No Parking' sign.

Her gaze flew to his. 'I see it.'

He smiled thinly. 'It's mine.'

'How charming. Am I supposed to applaud, or what?'

She saw a tiny vein throb in his temple. 'Walk to the curb and get into that car,' he said.

'Walk to the curb and...' Brionny tossed back her head and laughed. 'What do you think this is, Mc-Clintoch, a *Godfather* movie? You don't give orders to—Hey. Hey!' She grimaced as his hand clamped around her wrist and he began hustling her toward the car. 'What are you doing?'

'What does it look like I'm doing?' he said grimly.

Brionny slammed her fist against his shoulder.

'I'll scream!'

'Be my guest,' Slade growled. He held her tight against him, opened the car door, and thrust her into the passenger seat. 'Scream your head off. This is New York, remember? Nobody will notice—and if they do they'll pretend they didn't.'

Brionny glared at him. 'What's the reason for this, McClintoch? Have you gone from theft to kidnapping?'

His eyes narrowed. 'I suppose you'd have no trouble believing that.'

'You're damned right. You're capable of anything, and we both—'

His kiss silenced her in mid-sentence and landed, hard, on her parted lips.

Caught by surprise, she had no time to turn away. There was time only for her to feel the firmness of his mouth, the coolness of it—and to realize, with absolute horror, that she had not forgotten anything of how it felt to have his lips on hers.

'Do you really want to recover the Eye of God?' he asked softly.

Brionny licked her lips, trying not to notice the taste of him that now lay sweet on her tongue.

'Of—of course,' she said.

He smiled. 'I have a proposition to make to you, Bree, one I'm certain you'll find interesting.'

His voice was soft, almost husky. Her throat worked as she swallowed. 'What—what sort of proposition?'

He smiled. It was the same sexy smile he'd given her the time they'd first met, a lifetime ago, in the Hotel Florinda.

'I'll tell you all about it if you come with me quietly.'

'You're crazy, McClintoch. Why would I go with you any way at all?'

His smile grew even more intimate. 'I can think of at least two reasons. One, your boss handed you over to me for an indefinite period of time.'

'He didn't "hand me over" to you,' she said indignantly. 'I'm not your property!'

'Two,' he said calmly, 'it's the only way you're going to hear what I have to say.'

'I know what you have to say!'

'Yes. It's one of your finer qualities, Stuart. Knowing things in advance, I mean.'

Brionny folded her arms. 'What's the sense in playing games? There's no need for us to make a big thing out of this. You have a proposition to make to me—make it.'

'Aren't you even going to ask me if the Eye is safe?'

She blew a strand of hair off her forehead. 'Is it?'

He grinned. 'Safer than it was in that tampon box.'

She knew she was blushing but she kept her gaze steady on his.

'I'm not authorized to make any deals.'

'Deals?'

'You know what I mean. I've no idea what Esterhaus is willing to pay for the stone's return. You'll have to take it up with—'

'What if I told you I didn't want money for the stone?'

She stared at him. He was looking at her in a way that made her dizzy. His emerald eyes were hot, like flames; it was insane, but she could almost feel the lick of heat against her skin.

There was a strange knot of tension forming in the pit of her stomach. She'd felt like this standing at the edge of El Kaia Gorge in Slade's arms, almost overcome by a heady mixture of excitement and fear, the two mixed so closely together that it had been impossible to tell where one ended and the other began.

'I'd—I'd tell you to take it up with Esterhaus,' she said, 'not with me.'

Slade smiled, though the smile never reached his eyes. 'I don't think you'll want me to do that.'

'Well, you're wrong. That's just what I want.'

'You haven't even heard the proposition yet, but you're certain you want it dumped on the director's desk?'

She wasn't certain of anything except the bone-deep knowledge that she was being drawn into something way beyond her depth.

'Yes,' she said, 'I do.'

Slade shrugged. 'OK, Stuart. It's your choice.'

Quickly, before he could change his mind, Brionny swung her legs out of the car. Slade leaned toward her.

'Of course,' he said slyly, 'you realize we'll have to tell old Simon everything.'

'Exactly. Starting with the fact that you're the rotten crook who stole his emerald!'

Slade smiled. Her suit skirt had ridden well above her knees, and he was taking his time appreciating the view.

She tugged furiously at her hem.

'Don't do that,' she snapped.

His eyes met hers. 'Why not?' he said pleasantly. 'After all, we're going to get into much more intimate detail in Esterhaus's office. You want to tell him everything? Fine. I'll tell him all he needs to know—including the fact that you told me where to find the Eye of God after we'd made love.'

Color rose beneath Brionny's skin. 'He doesn't need to know that at all! And—we didn't make love. You seduced me, McClintoch, so you could steal that emerald!'

'We can leave out some of the more intimate details, I guess.' He ran his finger down her cheek. His eyes had gone dark, as silken-soft as his voice. 'Those little sounds you made when I kissed your breasts, or the way you reached for me when you wanted me deep inside you again.'

Brionny twisted her face away from his hand. 'Esterhaus called you a gentleman,' she said, her voice trembling. 'But I don't think you even know the meaning of the word.'

Slade's voice hardened. 'You don't *think*? Come on Bree, you're usually a hell of a lot more positive than that. You're the expert on who and what I am, remember? You sized me up from day one.'

'The only thing I know about you is that you belong

in jail. And I'm not going to rest until that's where you are!'

'This is getting tiresome, Stuart. Make a decision, please. What's it going to be? Truth and confession time in the director's office—or a friendly little chat alone with me?'

Brionny looked at Slade without speaking. It was inconceivable that she'd ever, even for a moment, imagined feeling something for this man. He was everything she'd thought him to be and worse.

'This proposition of yours had better be worth hearing,' she snapped.

He laughed. 'It is. In fact, I suspect you'll find it fascinating.' He slammed her door, came around the car, and climbed in behind the wheel. 'I can hardly wait to hear your reaction.'

He hit a button on the console and the locks on the doors snicked down into place.

Trapped, Brionny thought, and the car shot into traffic.

'I'm not going in there!'

Slade had pulled into a drive outside one of Manhattan's priciest bits of real estate, and now Brionny was sitting with her arms crossed and an expression of defiance on her face.

'Don't be ridiculous. Of course you are.'

'You said we were going to a restaurant. You never mentioned a word about taking me to an apartment.'

'I said we were going to lunch, Stuart. The days when ladies swooned at the prospect of setting foot inside a man's home are long gone.'

She looked from him to the glass skyscraper and laughed.

'This is your home? Come on, McClintoch. You don't really expect me to believe this is where you live.'

'Frankly, I don't give a damn what you believe, as long as you don't give the doorman a scene to remember for the rest of his life.' His gaze flicked past her. 'Good afternoon, Hodges.'

A man in a blue and maroon uniform was looking in at them and smiling.

'Afternoon, Mr McClintoch.' He put his hand to the brim of his cap. 'Ma'am.'

The door swung open. Brionny sat still for a second, and then she muttered something under her breath, gave the doorman a bright smile, and stepped from the car.

Slade took her arm as he came up beside her. 'Would you ring the Golden Phoenix and ask them to deliver the meal I ordered, please, Hodges?'

'Don't bother, Hodges.' Both men looked at Brionny. Another falsely polite smile curved across her lips. 'I'm afraid I won't be staying long enough to eat.'

Slade's fingers bit into her arm but he nodded. 'You heard the lady, Hodges.' He kept a tight grip on her arm as he led her under the portico, through the elegant lobby, and into an elevator.

'Afraid I'll bolt and run?' she said sweetly.

The elevator doors slid shut, and he let go of her and lounged back against the wall of the car.

'Too bad you decided to pass on lunch,' he said pleasantly. 'The Golden Phoenix does a terrific Peking duck.'

'How nice for the Golden Phoenix.' Brionny smiled tightly. 'But I don't care much for private luncheons.'

Slade breathed out a weary sigh. 'I know what you're thinking, and you can relax. Seduction isn't on the menu.'

'You've no idea what I'm thinking,' she said, her eyes fixed on the flashing floor numbers. 'It's your safety I had in mind, Slade, not mine. With witnesses around, I'd be less likely to shove you out the nearest win—'

The doors slid open, and she caught her breath in shock.

A marble entry foyer as large as Simon Esterhaus's office stretched ahead. Beyond it was a living-room almost the size of the museum's Great Hall.

'Whose apartment is this?' she whispered.

Slade laughed. 'Don't you mean, are we going to be arrested between dessert and coffee?' He tossed his car keys on a table and moved past her. 'What would you say if I told you it was mine?'

'I'd ask what bank you'd robbed,' Brionny said drily, 'and, in your case, it probably wouldn't be a joke.'

He smiled. 'Let's just say it's mine to use whenever I'm in New York.'

'It belongs to someone you know?'

'Yes. That's right. It belongs to someone I know.'

'Well, it's certainly nice to have friends who live in the right places.' She walked to a wall of glass that looked out over the East River. 'That's an impressive view.'

Slade shrugged his shoulders. 'It's OK. I prefer my place in Connecticut. Trees, rolling hills—'

'Is that where you live? Connecticut?'

'Why do you sound so surprised, Stuart?'

'I don't. I just—' Brionny looked at him. She had never thought of him living anywhere, she realized; she'd imagined him bouncing from country to country with no real place to call his own. And yet she had no difficulty picturing him in a sleek, contemporary house on a verdant hillside in Connecticut; he didn't even seem out of place here, in this apartment that might have come off the pages of *Better Homes and Gardens*...

'How about some wine?'

She blinked. Slade was holding out a glass half filled with a dark, ruby liquid. She hesitated, then took it from him. She didn't want the wine, but she did want something to hold on to, something that would make her feel less as if she was walking through a surrealistic dream.

'So.' Slade sipped his wine, then smiled. 'Do you really like my—my friend's apartment?'

Brionny nodded. 'I like the things he collects, too.' She nodded toward a series of glass shelves that housed a dozen or more tiny terracotta figures. 'I've never seen so many of those under one roof.'

'They're just clay,' Slade said lazily.

'They're pre-Colombian relics and worth a fortune. You probably don't...' She fell silent, and he chuckled.

'Ah, Stuart, you have a face that's so easy to read! You're sorry you said that. Now you're afraid I'm going to toss the figures into a suitcase and steal them!'

Faint spots of color rose in her cheeks. 'You knew they were valuable,' she said stiffly.

Slade grinned. 'Did I?'

'It doesn't matter to me if you steal everything in this place. Come to think of it, everything's probably stolen to begin with. Your pal most likely collects black market antiquities.'

'Really.'

She looked around the room, at the small Van Gogh on the far wall, the Klee over the fireplace, at the Egyptian cat that guarded a shelf displaying exquisite jade figures.

'My God,' she whispered, 'there's a king's ransom here!'

'And all of it stolen?' Slade asked politely.

Brionny glared at him. 'You think it's funny, don't you?'

Amusement fell from his face like a discarded mask. 'I think it's incredible how you set yourself up as judge and jury. I promise you, Brionny, the man who lives here is not a thief.'

'You're a fine one to give character references, McClintoch. Not that it matters to me. I'm only interested in the Eye of God.'

'Isn't that the truth?' Slade said pleasantly.

Brionny swung toward him. 'You said you had a proposition to make me, McClintoch. Suppose we get to it?'

He nodded, his eyes suddenly cool. 'I agree. The sooner we can agree on terms the better.'

Terms? Brionny thought. What did he mean? He couldn't really think she'd believed him when he'd said he didn't want money for the emerald. Of course he wanted money. Why else would he have stolen it in the first place?

Why was he being so mysterious? And why had he involved her? Was it because he figured he could trust her not to turn him in, that she had no choice but to do his bidding in order to protect herself?

Slade poured himself more wine. He took a drink, then looked at her.

'My price is non-negotiable.'

She nodded. 'I expected it would be. Well, I can't promise anything—'

A crooked smile eased across his lips. 'You'll have to.'

'I don't have the authority. Esterhaus didn't—'

'I told you, Esterhaus hasn't got a thing to do with this.' Slade put down his glass and walked toward her.

'If you knew the slightest thing about how museums operate, you wouldn't say that. Esterhaus is the only one with the power to approve whatever amount of money you request.'

He took her wineglass from her fingers and set it aside.

'You really weren't paying attention before, Stuart. I said I don't want money for the emerald.'

'Of course you do,' Brionny said, a little breathlessly. Why was he standing so close to her? 'Otherwise—'

'That's a hell of a habit,' he said softly. He smiled and stroked his thumb lightly across the fullness of her mouth. 'You're always so positive you know what I want—but you never bother checking with me to see if you're right.'

His touch scalded her. She wanted to move away from it, but where was there to go? The table was at her back, and Slade—Slade was so close that she could see that his eyes had turned a heated mix of turquoise, emerald and jade.

'And you're always right, aren't you, Bree?' His voice fell to a whisper. 'Just as you were right to have me locked in a roach-infested cell in Italpa—because I'd stolen your precious Eye.'

That he'd been locked up by the Italpan police was a shock. She waited for the elation that should have followed it, but all she felt was a strange hollowness.

'I didn't think they'd even filed my report. How—how did you make them let you go? Did you bribe them?'

His mouth twisted. 'Why ask me? You already know the answers you want to hear.'

His thumb was still moving gently against her flesh. She jerked away from his touch.

'Don't do that!'

'Why?' His smile was chill. 'Does it make you remember things you'd rather forget?'

'It makes me remember how much I dislike you,' she said sharply. 'Now, can we please get down to business?'

Slade stepped back. He tucked his hands into his trouser pockets, and walked slowly to the window.

'You want to know what price I've set on the emerald,' he said.

Brionny nodded. 'Yes.'

He swung around and smiled. 'Nothing you can't afford, Stuart.'

'It's not a matter of what I can or can't afford, Slade. The museum—'

'But it is,' he said. His smile vanished. 'You're going to buy the stone from me. Not Esterhaus or the museum.'

She laughed. 'Me? I haven't got the money to—'

'I'm not talking dollars.'

'You're not?' Why was her heart beginning to pound? Why was he looking at her like that, as if he were a cat and she were a canary, trapped in a cage with a paw-sized opening?

'The Mali-Mali barter for the things they want. You must know that.'

'The Mali-Mali!' Brionny's eyes flashed. 'Let's not talk about them, McClintoch, not if you want me to be in the right mood to listen to your so-called proposition.'

He showed his teeth in a quick smile. 'I'm just giving you some background, so you'll understand that what I'm about to suggest has historical validity.'

Brionny flung her hands on to her hips. 'Dammit, will you get to the point?'

'Here it is, then, Stuart.' He paused, and she found herself holding her breath, waiting for him to speak. 'We're going to barter, you and I. I give you the emerald—and you give me one night.'

It was a joke. It had to be a joke.

But Slade wasn't laughing. He wasn't even smiling any more.

Brionny shook her head. 'You're crazy!'

'It will all be very civilized. Dinner, dancing, a pleasant evening on the town—'

'You can't really mean this, Slade.'

'That's the price, lady. Take it or leave it.'

'But—but why?'

His mouth twisted. 'You always know what I'm up to, Stuart; figure it out for yourself.'

Brionny snatched up her purse and started past him. 'I won't even dignify this with an answer.'

'The hell you won't,' Slade growled, catching her by the arm. 'You'll survive the deal. You might even enjoy it. Think about the night we spent in that jungle shack.'

Heat swept into her cheeks. 'That night was an obscenity! If you hadn't lied to me about the danger we were supposed to be in—'

'I see.' His voice was soft as velvet. 'It was fear that drove you into my arms, hmm?'

'You know it was!' Humiliation made her reckless. 'Nothing else would have made me sleep with a man like you!'

She saw his face and wanted to call the words back,

but it was too late. Slade said something ugly, pulled her into his arms, and crushed her mouth under his. When he let her go, Brionny wiped the back of her hand across her lips.

'I only wish the headhunters had been real,' she said, her voice trembling, 'so they could have put an arrow through your heart. Why does it mean so much to you to humiliate me?'

Slade looked at her for a long moment, and then he turned and stood with his back to her, his gaze riveted on the scene below.

'You're beginning to bore me, Stuart,' he said. 'Do we have a deal or not?'

Brionny closed her eyes. She thought of Professor Ingram, who'd given his life for the Eye of God. She thought of the generations of Indians who had worshipped it. She thought of the long line of archaeologists standing like watchful, ancestral shadows behind her.

And she thought of the one person responsible for the emerald's loss, the one person who now had the chance to set things right...

Slade turned to her. 'Well?' he demanded impatiently. 'Is it yes—or is it no?'

A shudder went through her. She took a deep, deep breath and said the only thing she could.

She said yes.

CHAPTER TEN

BRIONNY STARED at her reflection in her bedroom mirror.

Her dress was midnight-blue lace, an expensive bit of gossamer she'd bought on impulse at a sale months before and never worn. It had thin straps and a short, above-the-knee skirt. Sterling silver hoops swayed from her earlobes; a silver chain glinted against the soft, rising curve of her breasts. On her feet were slender-heeled silver sandals.

She looked as if she was dressed for a special date with a special man. Her throat closed. In truth, she was dressed for a charade.

At least she'd realized that truth before the night began.

She thought back to what had happened this afternoon. Within seconds after she'd caved in to Slade's ugly demand, she'd known she couldn't go through with it. She hated herself for it, but at least she'd gone to him willingly that first time. But selling herself to him—that was different. The price was too high, no matter what the pay-off.

She'd turned to him to tell him that, but Slade had spoken first.

'You disappoint me, sweetheart,' he'd said slowly. 'I expected a lecture on my lack of morality, or an appeal to my better nature. And how about some girlish tears? A desperate plea for compassion?'

And, in that moment, she'd realized that it was all a sham. He would never give her the emerald. It was worth far too much money and he'd risked too much to get it.

Slade was lying, but there was nothing new in that. Lying was what he did best. He'd set up this whole ugly little exercise to make her pay for the night he'd spent in jail in Italpa.

The realization had sent a swift, fierce sense of power sweeping through her. Knowing his game, she could afford to play it—but by her own rules.

She would turn the game back on him. She had already taken the first step, even though it had been by pure good luck.

Accepting his obscene offer—seeming to accept it, anyway—had denied him the pleasure of watching her grovel. Now she'd deny him everything else.

And so she'd squared her shoulders, looked straight into his cold, lying eyes, and told him that people like her never pleaded for anything.

It had been the perfect exit line. She'd stalked out, head high—and between then and now she'd planned her strategy.

She would go out with him this evening. She would be polite and proper—so polite and proper that it would make his head spin. But she would never miss the chance to insult him—as politely as possible, of course. And when the end of the night came, if he was fool enough to try and take her in his arms, she would tell him that he wasn't the only one who could lie through his teeth and get away with it.

'You must be crazy,' she'd say. 'I wouldn't sleep with you if you offered me the Hope diamond.'

And then she'd offer him her own proposition. He could hand over the emerald to her and she'd keep his secret. She'd tell no one that Slade McClintoch was a thief.

If not, she'd turn him over to Esterhaus.

How stupid she'd been, thinking Slade could blackmail her! What he held over her head was nothing compared to what she could tell the world about him.

He was the one with everything to lose, not she. It had taken her a while to figure it out, but now that she had—

The doorbell sounded. Brionny's heart gave a fluttering beat.

Was it really time already?

She took a deep breath and made her way through the living-room.

Be polite, she reminded herself, be chillingly polite, and she flung the door open like a queen greeting her subjects.

'Good evening,' she said. 'You're right on—'

The words died on her lips. Slade was wearing a black dinner suit that had surely been custom-tailored to make the most of his height, his powerful shoulders, his hard, lean body. The white ruffled shirt beneath the jacket set off his tanned, angular face, the softness of the ruffles somehow enhancing the overall aura of masculinity that surrounded him.

'Good evening.' His gaze moved slowly over her before returning to her face. 'You look beautiful.'

Brionny pulled herself together and managed a brittle smile. 'Really?' she said. 'This old thing? It's terribly out of date.'

'These are for you.' He held out a nosegay of flowers, a magnificent riot of reds, corals and pinks. 'The color choice was sheer luck, but I'm glad to see it complements your dress.'

It would have complemented anything, she thought, her fingers itching with the desire to touch the lovely blossoms. Instead, she shook her head.

'How unfortunate. I'm afraid I don't like flowers, Slade. I'm allergic to them.'

His eyes narrowed, as if he was slowly catching on to what was happening.

'What a shame,' he said.

'Yes, isn't it?'

'It must have been hell for you, down there in the Amazon. Traipsing through a jungle filled with all sorts of flowers, I mean.'

'Oh, it was. Except for the time I spent with Professor Ingram, my entire stay in the Amazon was hell.'

Slade's lips drew back from his teeth. 'Nicely done, Stuart.'

Her smile was the equal of his. 'Thank you,' she purred.

She took her purse from the table. You don't know the half of it, McClintoch, she thought, and swept past him.

It was going to be one hell of a night.

Slade's red sports car wove swiftly in and out of traffic.

Where were they going? Not to the apartment he was staying in; they'd left Manhattan behind half an hour ago. Now they were speeding along a highway that traveled the length of Long Island.

Damn, but the silence in the car was oppressive. She

was tempted to ask Slade to put on some music, but—

As if on signal, he reached toward the built-in compact-disk player, hit a button, and the poignant strains of a Rachmaninoff piano concerto filled the car. She almost laughed. A man like him, pretending to like such rich, romantic music? Who was he trying to impress?

'Is Rachmaninoff OK?' he said.

Brionny folded her hands in her lap. 'If you like that sort of thing.'

'You don't?'

Of course she did. She always had. But that wasn't the point, not tonight.

'His work's been played to death.' She gave him a polite little smile. 'What CD is that? One of those things they sell on TV, "Rachmaninoff's Ten Greatest Hits"?'

To her surprise, he laughed.

'"The Best of Bach", you mean, or "Beethoven's Hit Parade"?' He flexed his hands on the steering wheel. 'Those old boys would spin in their graves if they knew how their stuff's marketed today—they'd spin at 78 RPM, of course.'

Brionny stared at him. She wanted to laugh—it was a funny line, and it evoked a funny picture. In fact, she almost did laugh. But at the last second, thank goodness, she remembered that she couldn't.

Slade pulled the disk from the player. 'Let's try something brighter. How about Vivaldi?'

Vivaldi. Her favorite composer. Such beautiful, lyrical music...

'Every film maker for the last ten years seems to have used Vivaldi,' she said, flashing him another chill smile. 'Not that I blame them. Vivaldi's music is so—so accessible.'

The arrow seemed to have missed its target. Slade simply shrugged.

'Choose something you prefer, then. There are other CDs in the glove compartment.'

Well, she'd walked right into that. Brionny sighed and popped open the compartment door.

'I'm sure you'll find something you like. I have fairly eclectic taste.'

'Eclectic' wasn't the word for it. Her eyebrows rose as she shuffled through the disks. The Beatles. Borodin. Eric Clapton. Gershwin. Billie Holliday...

'Billie Holliday?' she said aloud, before she could stop herself.

Slade glanced at her. 'You probably never heard of the lady. She was a blues singer a long time back, maybe the greatest that—'

'—Ever lived.' Brionny bit her lip. 'I—uh—I know.'

Damn. Why was she talking so much? She stabbed the CD into the slot. Billie Holliday's soft, quavering voice drifted from the speakers.

'Do you like jazz, Stuart?'

No harm in answering that.

'Yes.'

'All kinds?'

Of course, all kinds.

'I never thought about it,' she said.

'Modern?'

Well, maybe not modern. Too much of the music seemed self-indulgent. Unless it was Miles Davis or Chet Baker—

'I don't,' Slade said, without waiting for her to answer. 'Care for most of the modern stuff, I mean. Unless it's Davis or Baker, I get bored with all those self-serving riffs.'

Brionny swung her head toward him. Was it some sort of parlor trick, this seeming ability to read her mind?

No, of course it wasn't. She turned away, looked out into the night. Lots of people liked jazz. It just seemed surprising that Slade would—

'I'm surprised you like jazz, Stuart.'

'Are you?' she said, as if the question were too dull to consider.

'Well, it's so unstructured.' Slade flashed her a quick smile. 'I'd have thought you'd prefer—'

'It isn't. It only seems that way if you don't understand it.'

Slade nodded. 'I agree. I met this guy once—'

What did she care whom he'd met? And how had she let herself get drawn into this foolish conversation?

From now on, she'd be silent.

'...Club Blue Note. Ever been there?'

Once. The night had been a fiasco. The club had been wonderful, smoky and dark just like the music coming from the tiny bandstand, but her date had despised it. Too crowded, he'd said, and the noise was awful.

'Once,' she said. 'It was crowded, and the noise was awful.'

'You're probably right. Anyway, the place to go, if you want to hear the best blues, is the old Chicago Red Slipper.'

'Oh, have you really been to the Red Slipper? I've read about it, but—'

Brionny flushed, clamped her lips together, and turned away.

'But what?'

'Nothing,' she said, very coldly.

'Come on, Stuart. What were you going to say?'

'This wasn't part of the deal,' she said, even more coldly. 'All this—this silly chitchat...'

'I'm writing the rules tonight, Bree.' His voice was soft, but she could hear the steel in it.

'You didn't say you expected conversation, Slade, only that you expected—'

The tires squealed as he turned the wheel sharply and brought the car to a sudden stop on the shoulder of the road.

'Behave yourself,' he warned. He reached to her and curled his fingers around the nape of her neck. 'Otherwise the deal's off. Understand?'

The deal's off anyway, Brionny thought, and she smiled.

'Certainly,' she said.

Slowly, his hand fell away from her. He took a deep breath and clamped his fingers around the steering wheel.

'I made reservations at a place on the North Shore of the island. Five stars, elegant décor, *boeuf en croute*, a pair of violinists playing softly in the background...'

'Are you waiting for me to tell you it sounds wonderful?'

'I've been there a dozen times. The food's always excellent, the music's unobtrusive, and the service is impeccable.' He reached for her hand. She almost yanked it back, then she decided it would be better to let it lie boneless in his. 'But I know this little place on the ocean,' he murmured, his fingers lacing through hers. 'They serve the best ribs and jazz this side of the Mason-Dixon line. How does that sound?'

Like a place a man would take a woman on a real date, Brionny thought, and a tremor went through her.

Slade brought her hand to his lips. She caught her breath as his mouth grazed her skin.

'We'll go there instead,' he said. 'You'll like it.' He put her hand back into her lap and stepped on the gas.

It was, as he'd said, a little place by the sea.

What he hadn't said was that he was taking her to an old Victorian house with a widow's walk and lots of gingerbread outside, and wonderful smells and overflowing baskets of flowers inside.

This was no out-of-the-way café. It was an expensive hideaway its devotees had protected from the food critics, and you probably needed to make reservations weeks in advance—and then hope they might be honored.

The hostess, a small black woman with skin the color of rich coffee and a broad, generous smile, saw Slade as soon as he and Brionny entered. She came sailing through the line of people waiting to be seated and threw her arms around him.

'Ellen,' he said, kissing her cheek.

'Slade.' Her voice was as Southern, as soft as a ripe Georgia peach. 'We haven't seen you in months.'

'This is Brionny Stuart. I've told her you've got the best food and the best music in the world.'

Ellen laughed as she shook Brionny's hand. 'He exaggerates,' she said. 'The best in this hemisphere—I'm not sure about the world.'

She led them to a table beside a window, with a view out over the moonlit ocean.

'Now,' Ellen said, plucking the 'reserved' sign from the center of the table, 'let me tell this young lady what to order.'

Slade grinned. 'Ellen wants to make sure you don't get the wrong idea and think this place is a democracy.'

Brionny smiled politely. 'That's all right,' she said. 'I'm really not very—'

'Nonsense,' Ellen said briskly. 'Of course you're hungry. And you'll eat. No one comes to Ellen's Place without eating. The food's much too good for that.'

'Well, I—'

'You can't be dieting,' Ellen said, eyeing Brionny critically. 'You're too thin as it is. So what's the problem, child? Are you piqued at something this big man did?'

Brionny's cheeks colored. 'No, no, of course not. I just—'

'The fried chicken is delicious, and so are the barbecued beef and the pork ribs. You'll have to try all three, and then you'll have some Creole coffee and a slab of my sweet potato pie.' Ellen softened her command with a grin. 'Don't panic. I'll tell the kitchen to send out small portions.' She patted Brionny's shoulder, waggled her fingers at Slade, and hurried off.

Brionny looked at Slade. 'Is she always so reserved?'

He grinned. 'She's not kidding, you know. She'll come back and scold you if you don't clean your plate.' He leaned forward, his eyes on hers. 'Well, what do you think?'

She looked around. Their table was very private, set with a blue and white checked cloth, heavy white napkins and handsome silver flatware. It was lit by the soft glow of a candle in a crystal holder. Across the room, on a small bandstand, a handful of men in tuxedos were playing the sweetest, most wonderful blues she'd ever heard.

This was a magical place, a marvelous place...

'Bree? Do you like it?'

She swallowed. 'It's—very nice.'

'Very nice, huh?' Slade smiled. 'See if you can stay with that lukewarm description after we've been here a while.'

She tried. She really did. But how could she? The food was ambrosial. The music was superb. And Slade—Slade was—

He was a man she had never met before.

He knew which ale went best with ribs, which wine would complement the chicken. He knew the names of the tongue-twisting spices that had lent depth and smokiness to the dark, rich beef, and the intricacies between one kind of barbecue technique and the next.

Over the chicken, he told her a story about Machu Pichu that made her smile. Over the ribs, he told her how he'd once confused the Japanese words *tatami* and *tisumi* with near-disastrous results, and made her laugh. Over the beef, he told her how he'd almost been thrown out of Boston University for a night that started with too much beer and ended with twenty fraternity brothers making a drunken, naked dash into a snow bank.

She didn't smile or laugh. She just stared at him.

'You went to Boston University?'

Slade's smile was stilted. 'An illusion shot to hell, Stuart? You figured me for a high-school dropout.'

It was the perfect time to say yes, that was precisely what she'd figured—but she couldn't.

'Actually—actually, I never thought about it.'

'It's OK. My mother had that same look on her face when I told her I'd wangled myself a scholarship. Nobody in our family had ever taken a university degree; I think she'd have accepted it better if I'd told her I was going to be the first McClintoch to go to the moon.'

He was still smiling, but there was a tension between them again. It was just as well, Brionny thought; for a little while, she'd almost forgotten why she was with Slade tonight; she'd almost forgotten what sort of deal they'd made, what she intended to do...

He reached out and touched his forefinger lightly to the corner of her mouth. His touch sizzled against her skin and she jerked back.

'Just being helpful,' he said. 'You had a spot of sauce on your lip.'

She stared at him, her pulse suddenly racing in her throat. He smiled, pushed back his chair, and rose to his feet.

'Come,' he said softly.

He was holding out his hand and moving in rhythm with the soft Gershwin tune the band was playing.

'No,' she said quickly, 'I don't—'

Slade reached for her, and before she could figure out a way to stop it from happening she was in his arms.

She didn't want him to hold her so close, but the floor was small and crowded. His hand came up and cupped her head, and he tucked her face into the curve of his shoulder.

Brionny's eyes closed. The feel of him, the smell of him were so painfully familiar. Memories flooded her senses: she knew his hair would be silken under her fingers, knew his skin would taste salty and warm.

God, she thought, oh, God, if only this were real...

What was the matter with her? This could never be real. She hated Slade, hated everything he stood for...

'Bree.' His mouth was at her temple; she could feel the soft whisper of his breath against her hair. 'Bree—I have to tell you something.'

What could he possibly tell her? More lies, she

thought, and she began to tremble. Soft, sweet lies this time, judging by the way he was holding her, by the way his hands were moving softly along her spine, lies he hoped would draw her down into a whirlpool of desire and give the evening the perfect finish.

But it wouldn't happen. And it was time he knew it.

'Bree,' he whispered, and she yanked herself out of his arms and looked at him.

'I want to go home.'

'Now?' There was bewilderment in his green eyes. 'But it's still early.'

'No, it's not,' she said. 'It's late. Later than you ever imagined.'

She started to turn away and Slade reached for her, caught her by the shoulder harder than he'd intended, and swung her toward him. People around them on the tiny floor cast sidelong looks, but he didn't notice.

'No,' he said sharply, 'no, you're not leaving, dammit. You're going to listen.'

'To you?' She laughed. 'What could a man like you possibly say that a woman like me would want to hear?'

Behind him, someone gave a muffled giggle. Slade spun toward the sound, his cheeks flushed, but no one met his eyes. When he looked for her again, Brionny was stalking from the dance floor.

Damn her! And damn him, for having thought she'd seen him, really seen him, for the first time, for having been about to tell her everything—who he was, what had really happened to her precious emerald...

He drew a breath. She had saved him from making a complete ass of himself, he thought grimly. He owed her something for that.

He reached the table an instant after she did, peeled

some bills from his wallet, and dropped them on the cloth.

'Let's go,' he growled, and he took her arm. She made a little sound and he knew he was hurting her but he didn't much care. Out of the corner of his eye he saw Ellen staring at him, but he didn't much care about that either.

The heat in the parking lot was oppressive. Beside him, Brionny was trying to break his hold, but she didn't have a chance.

What a fool he'd made of himself tonight! Determined to humble Brionny Stuart, convinced he owed her a lesson for the pain she'd inflicted on him, he'd forced her into an unholy contract and then ended up trying to please her instead.

How in hell could one woman who stood for everything he despised always end up making him lose his self-control?

'I'm speaking to you, McClintoch!'

He looked at her. They had reached his car; he was holding her against it and she was looking at him through eyes that blazed with contempt.

'Forgive me, my lady,' he said. His teeth glinted in a shark-like smile. 'I didn't hear you.'

'I said I'd rather go home by taxi.'

'Would you?'

'Yes. This night is at an end.'

Slade laughed. He opened the car door and pushed her inside.

'No,' he said, very softly, 'no, sweetheart, it is not.'

She was frightened now; he could see it in her face, although she was doing her best not to show it. Quickly, he got behind the wheel, put the car in gear, and sent it sliding out of the gravel lot.

She swung her head toward him. His profile was blade-sharp, his mouth thin. Her hands shook a little, and she folded them quickly into her lap.

'This display of machismo is boring,' she said. Her voice, at least, was steady. 'And it's not impressive.'

'I'm not interested in impressing you, Bree.' He looked at her, his smile terrifying in its emptiness. 'We made a deal, remember?'

'The deal's off,' she said sharply.

'Don't be silly, sweetheart. Don't you want that emerald?'

'Why don't you tell the truth for once, Slade? You just wanted to—to bring me to my knees. You know it's money you want for the emerald, not me.'

'Ah,' he said, 'Brionny Stuart, she who knows all, speaks again!' His voice hardened, became like the sting of a whip. 'Well, you're wrong, lady. We made a deal, and you're going to live with it. You're spending the night with me.'

'Slade, damn you—'

He reached out, dumped the Billie Holliday CD from the player, stabbed in the Rachmaninoff, and turned up the volume. Music, loud and dramatic, filled the car with sound. Speech was impossible.

Brionny gritted her teeth. She hadn't pleaded this afternoon; that was what this was all about. He wanted her to plead now.

She'd sooner burn in hell.

Let him put on an act. He was angry, he was trying to scare her, but so what? No matter what else he was, Slade was not a man who would force a woman into his bed.

Cars lined the curb in front of her apartment building. Slade shot into a space beside a fire hydrant. He slammed his way out of the car, clamped his hand around Brionny's wrist, and marched her up the four flights of steps to her apartment.

'The key,' he demanded, holding out his palm. When she didn't move, he pushed her back against the door, took her purse from her and dug through it until he'd found what he wanted. Then he undid the lock and shoved her inside.

He's trying to scare me, Brionny told herself, that's all he's doing.

When he unbuttoned his dinner jacket and dropped it across the back of the sofa, she decided things had gone far enough.

'That's it,' she said. 'You've made your point. You're stronger than I am, and—'

He laughed. 'Haven't we had this conversation before, sweetheart?' He reached out and took hold of her shoulders. 'Don't fight me, Bree. I don't want to hurt you.'

At last, fear flooded through her veins. 'No,' she said. 'Slade, don't—'

His kiss was punishing and painful, forced on her unwilling mouth with a pressure that made her head fall back.

'Stop it,' she panted, struggling frantically against him.

'Hell, sweetheart, I'm disappointed. I thought ladies of your class never tried to squirm out of an agreement.'

She cried out as he kissed her again, his mouth fierce and hot.

'You're hurting me! Slade, please…'

All at once, the terror in her voice cut through the blind rage that had almost overcome him.

He went absolutely still. 'Bree?' he said. 'Bree…'

His eyes swept over her face. He saw the tears on her lashes, saw her mouth, bruised and swollen from his kisses. He looked at her arms, at his fingers biting deep into her flesh, and he groaned with despair.

'Dear God,' he said. 'Bree, sweetheart, forgive me!'

He gathered her to him, pressing soft kisses to her hair, to her throat. He murmured her name, over and over, and stroked his hands over her back.

'I'm sorry,' he whispered, 'I'm so sorry...'

With a little sob of desperation, her arms went around his neck. She brought his head down to hers and kissed him, her mouth open to his. She didn't understand it, but fear had given way to something else, something that was always there when she was in Slade's arms, a desire so sharp and sweet it was like a pain in her heart.

The emerald, she thought as his hands began moving over her, the damned emerald! If only he'd really give it to her, she could return it to Esterhaus along with some made-up story about how she'd come by it, and all this would be behind them. There would be time to explore these feelings, this incredible, wonderful emotion she'd felt ever since she'd met him...

'Bree.' Slade kissed her deeply. 'I have to tell you...' She moved in his arms, just enough to lean back and look up at him. The action sent her hips against his and he groaned and shifted his aroused body against hers. 'Hell, it's going to have to wait.'

'No,' she said urgently, 'it can't wait. I have to talk to you, Slade.'

He swallowed hard, took a breath, and took a step back.

'You're right. This conversation is long overdue.'

Brionny put her fingers over his lips. 'Don't say anything until you've heard what I have to say. Please.'

He gave a choked laugh. 'Hell, we'll have to take turns. OK, sweetheart. You first.'

She drew a deep, steadying breath into her lungs. 'Slade? Did you mean it when you said you'd give me the Eye of God?'

He tensed. 'The emerald? That's what you want to talk about?'

'Yes! Of course. It's the most important thing we—'

'Sure it is.' Slade looked at her, at the soft mouth and beautiful eyes that offered a promise of warmth that was a lie, and he felt a coldness seeping into his bones. 'Business before pleasure, right?'

Brionny's face paled. 'You don't understand.'

'But I do.' He let go of her, knowing that if he didn't he might put his hands around her lovely, fragile throat and squeeze. 'I understand completely—and because you made the evening interesting I'll even give you an honest answer.' His eyes, flat and bright as green glass, met hers. 'I never had any intention of giving you the emerald, sweetheart.' His lips drew back from his teeth. 'A night with you, for the Eye of God? Not even the Mali-Mali would have made such a poor trade.'

Slade picked up his jacket, flung it over his shoulder, and walked out into the night.

CHAPTER ELEVEN

EARLY IN the morning, the museum was so quiet that Brionny's footsteps seemed to echo like gunshots as she made her way through the Great Hall.

She had always liked the museum at this time, just before the crowds invaded. One of the privileges of being on staff was that you could flash your ID at the guard at the gate and enter the building early, either for some quiet time at your desk or simply to stroll the halls and enjoy the treasures of the world in privacy.

That was what she was doing now, taking a last, peaceful look at the artifacts she loved, because she knew that the next time she came to this museum it would be as a paying patron.

But it would be worth it. By this time tomorrow, the museum would have its emerald.

And Slade would be where he belonged, in a prison cell.

At seven, she'd telephoned Simon Esterhaus at his home. His voice had been muzzy with sleep and gruff with the displeasure of being awakened. After she'd identified herself, his tone had sharpened.

'Have you news of the emerald, Miss Stuart?' he'd said.

Brionny had taken a deep, deep breath.

'I know who has it, sir.'

'Wonderful!' Esterhaus's joy had been almost palpable. 'That's wonderful news, my dear. Tell me everything.'

'I will, Mr Esterhaus. But—but not over the telephone.'

'Of course, Miss Stuart. I'll see you at ten. I take it Mr McClintoch will be with you?'

'No. He will not be with me, sir. I'll be alone.'

If that had struck Esterhaus as odd, he had not said so. Now, in just a few minutes, she would meet with him in his office—and this nightmare would finally come to an end.

She glanced at her watch, turned, and made her way slowly across the hall. The huge front doors were just opening and the early arrivals were filtering in. Students clutching notebooks, tourists, families with children whose squeals turned quickly to excited whispers when they spotted the impressive Tyrannosaurus Rex rearing up in the center of the Great Hall.

The anteroom to Esterhaus's office loomed ahead. Brionny came to an abrupt halt, her heart hammering. Then, before she could lose courage, she strode purposefully through the open door.

Esterhaus's secretary looked up from her desk.

'Good morning, Miss Stuart. The director is expecting you.'

Brionny tried to smile, but her lips felt stuck to her teeth. She nodded, marched to the door to Esterhaus's office, knocked lightly and opened it.

It was like a replay of her last appearance here. Esterhaus was seated at his desk, thumbing through a stack of papers. He looked up, frowned, and motioned her forward.

'Sit down, Miss Stuart.'

Brionny sat. She waited for him to say something more; when he didn't she cleared her throat.

'Mr Esterhaus. Sir. I—I have news about the Eye of God.'

Esterhaus took off his eyeglasses, massaged the bridge of his nose, and leaned back in his chair.

'Yes, so you said, Miss Stuart, but I think I should tell you—'

'Sir, please, this is—it's difficult for me to talk about. I'd appreciate it if you'd just let me—just let me say my piece. I'm sure you'll have questions, and I'm more than willing to answer them, but—but—'

Esterhaus sighed. 'Of course. Please, say whatever you wish.'

Brionny ran the tip of her tongue across her lips. She had gone over her speech dozens of times; it was the only thing that had kept her sane during the hours of the night.

She cleared her throat.

'Sir. You know—you know that there was a man traveling with me when the emerald was taken from me. And you know that—that I thought we were in grave danger from headhunters.'

'Miss Stuart—'

'The missionary thought I'd been hallucinating, but—'

'But he was wrong. The headhunters were dangerously real.'

Brionny blinked. 'No. They weren't real at all, Mr Esterhaus. Perhaps I didn't make that clear when we spoke, but—'

'An advisory reached me yesterday from Peru, Miss Stuart.' Esterhaus popped his glasses on his nose, thumbed through the papers on his desk and selected one. '"To Simon Esterhaus, Director,"' he read, '"from the Minister for...blah, blah, blah. Please be advised that permits for the purposes of archaeological and anthropological digs will be temporarily suspended due to..."'

He whipped off his glasses and looked at Brionny. 'The point of all this bureaucratic mumbo jumbo, Miss Stuart, is that some rarely seen Indian tribe's suddenly come creeping out of the jungle. The Mori-Mori, something like that.'

'The Mali-Mali?' Brionny said, eyes wide.

'That's it. Apparently they went on the warpath just about the time you located the Eye of God.'

She swallowed convulsively. 'Because the professor and I took the stone?'

'No, no, it's nothing to do with that.'

'The road, then. They must be angry about the road that's going through the jungle, and—'

'It's not that either. According to this directive, the— what did you call them?'

'The Mali-Mali,' Brionny whispered.

'The Mali-Mali are stirred up over some internal problem, a battle between two warring factions that's been broadened to include anyone who gets in their way.' His sharp little teeth showed in a quick smile. 'Primitive, but not without a certain definite parallel in our own world, don't you agree?'

Brionny sat back in her chair. Slade had not lied, then—at least, he had not lied about the headhunters. But he had lied about everything else—about wanting her, about trust, about caring...

'Miss Stuart?'

She blinked. 'Sir?'

'I was saying, if that's all you wanted to tell me—'

'No, it isn't. There's—there's more, Mr Esterhaus.'

The director sighed. 'Go on, then, Miss Stuart.'

'I—I think you have the right to know that I bear sole responsibility for the loss of the Eye of God, sir.'

Esterhaus's brows lifted. 'I thought you said it was stolen from you, by your traveling companion.'

'Yes. It was.' Brionny hesitated. The hard part was coming—and yet this wasn't the worst of it, not by a long shot. 'But—but he'd tried to get it from me before, many times.'

'Go on.'

She looked up. Esterhaus was watching her with a little smile on his face. Oh, God, she thought, God...

'I'd refused to tell him where it was, you see, because I knew—I knew he would steal it. And then, that last night...' Brionny took a shaky breath and stared past the director, her eyes focused on the wall. 'That last night, I made a terrible mistake. I told him where he could find the stone, I told him where I'd hidden it, and—and—'

Her voice broke. She gave a sob and buried her face in her hands.

Esterhaus shoved back his chair and hurried toward her. 'Miss Stuart, my dear young woman, you were under an incredible amount of stress. In the circumstances—'

'Dammit, Mr Esterhaus!' Brionny looked up, her eyes streaming. She dug into her pocket for a tissue, blotted her eyes, and blew her nose noisily. 'Will you please stop interrupting and let me get this over with?'

Esterhaus drew back. 'If that is what you wish, Miss Stuart, but I assure you it isn't necessary. If you'd just listen to me for a moment—'

'No,' she said fiercely, rising to her feet, '*you* listen

to *me*, sir! I have something to tell you, and, and—I know where the Eye of God is,' she said.

Esterhaus smiled politely. 'Go on.'

Brionny frowned. She'd certainly expected more of a reaction than that.

'It won't cost us a penny to recover it, because we won't have to buy it, you see; we'll only have to have the thief who took it arrested.'

'Miss Stuart—'

'Don't you want to know his name?'

'No, not really, Miss Stuart. You see—'

'What do you mean, ''not really''?' Her face, pale but for the slashes of color in her cheeks, took on a stern cast. 'I want the thief tried, convicted and imprisoned. I want him to spend years in jail. I want him to be old and feeble by the time he gets out.'

Esterhaus was smiling again, in a manner that was almost paternal.

'Ah,' he said. 'I think I'm beginning to understand.'

'Good,' Brionny said. 'You'd better understand. And you'd better be prepared to bring charges against— against—'

After a moment's silence, Esterhaus his throat. 'Against?'

Brionny stared at him. I can't tell him, she thought, I can't!

She had spent the endless hours of the night deciding which punishment Slade deserved more, immersion in boiling oil or being tied to the rack, reminding herself that she would have to be satisfied with seeing him handcuffed and led off to prison—and now, with her chance finally at hand, she couldn't do it. She couldn't condemn Slade to a cell and to years of confinement.

'Miss Stuart?' Esterhaus said gently.

Brionny looked at him, her eyes bright with unshed tears. 'I can't tell you,' she whispered.

'Well, then,' Esterhaus said, even more gently, 'if you can't tell me the thief's name, how will we recover the stone?'

She stared at him while her brain processed the question. It was a good question. An excellent one.

And she had no answer.

'I'll find a way,' she whispered, blotting at her eyes with the now useless tissue. 'I'll go to—to the thief, and—and I'll plead. I'll get down on my knees and beg him to give me the stone, so I can return it to you. I'll offer him anything, anything—'

'Anything, Bree?'

She spun around. Slade was standing in the doorway, dressed as if he were back in the jungle, in jeans and a cotton shirt and dusty, well-worn boots. His hands were on his hips, and he was watching her with absolutely no expression on his face.

'McClintoch,' Esterhaus said happily. Brionny watched as he hurried across the room and grasped Slade's hand. 'It's so good to see you.'

Slade smiled tightly. 'We only saw each other two hours ago, Simon,' he said, his eyes never leaving Brionny's face.

'Of course, of course.' Esterhaus laughed. 'But the man who gave the museum such a gift will always be a welcome visitor in my office.'

Brionny tried to speak, but her throat was dry. She forced moisture into her mouth, then swallowed.

'Gift?' she whispered. 'What gift?'

'I've been trying to tell you, Miss Stuart. The Eye of God is safe in the museum vault.'

'What? But how—?'

'Mr McClintoch telephoned me just after you did this morning. He told me that you and he had recovered the Eye of God.'

'He told you…?'

'He explained that the thief had agreed to return the emerald at no cost, provided we agreed to keep the matter quiet.' Esterhaus put his finger to his lips. 'I assured Mr McClintoch that there was no problem with that, of course.'

'Of course,' Brionny said lamely.

'It means,' Esterhaus said, smiling at her, 'that we will never know the name of the thief, nor even how he came by the stone—'

'But I told you that much,' Brionny whispered.

'Did you?' Esterhaus shook his head. 'I'm afraid I've so much on my mind this morning, Miss Stuart, that I wasn't paying full attention.' He looked from Slade to Brionny and cleared his throat. 'In fact, I have an appointment in just a few minutes, so if neither of you minds…'

'Neither of us minds,' Slade said, his eyes still on Brionny.

The door swung shut and they were alone.

Slade spoke first. 'I heard that last part,' he said as he walked slowly toward her. 'That you'd get down on your knees, if you had to, and beg the thief to give back the stone.'

Brionny flushed. 'Why do you sound surprised? You were the one who kept saying I'd do anything to get the Eye back.'

'Not quite. You didn't tell Esterhaus I was the man who'd stolen it.' He moved forward again until they were a breath apart. 'Why didn't you?'

'That's my business, McClintoch.'

He reached out and touched her hair, his hand gentle and light. 'For a woman who couldn't wait to have me locked up in Italpa, that's one heck of a change in attitude.'

Brionny moistened her lip with the tip of her tongue. 'Were there—were there really roaches in the Italpa jail?'

Slade smiled. 'Big enough to lasso, Stuart, but it was just as well. Trying to stomp them to death kept me from thinking about what I'd do to you when I saw you again.'

'What *you'd* do to *me*?' Brionny's voice rose with indignation. 'That's very funny McClintoch. You stole the emerald from me, and —'

'I took it from your pack while you were sleeping.'

'Damned right you did!'

'I took it because I woke up and heard the Mali-Mali drums in the jungle.'

Brionny's eyes widened. 'What?'

'I thought, If only I'd spent the last hours of daylight building a raft, we might have a chance.' A fleeting smile curved across his mouth. 'And then I thought, Hell, those hours with Bree in my arms were the best hours of my life. I figured if I had to die I was ready.' His eyes darkened. 'But I didn't want you to die, sweetheart. I decided there had to be a way to stop those bastards.'

Without thinking, Brionny put her hand out and touched Slade's arm.

'And?' she whispered. 'What did you do?'

'I took the emerald from your pack. I kissed you and stepped outside. Everything was still—even the sound of the river seemed muted. The drumming had stopped.'

He smiled again, but Brionny could see the tension in the smile. 'Not a good sign, I figured.'

'No,' she said, caught up in the story. 'No, I suppose not.'

'I had to do something and do it fast. So I rubbed myself all over with mud—for camouflage—and made my way through the trees. I ended up right in the middle of twenty or thirty Mali-Mali. I figured I was as good as dead anyway, so I stuck out my hand, let the rising sun glint off the Eye, and told the bastards to come and get it if they had the guts.'

Brionny stared at him. It was an incredible story, so unreal that if any other man had told it she'd have known it was an outright lie. But it was easy to picture Slade doing just what he'd said, going off to save her, daring the savages to take him on.

'The emerald and my head would probably be sitting in some Mali-Mali village this minute—except that the Indians went crazy when the light hit that stone. They leaped into the air, yelling like banshees. *''Woowie''*, somebody screamed, or something like that. It scared the hell out of me and I screamed back. The next thing I knew, they were racing off like the wind—What's so funny?'

'My God, Slade!' Brionny's shoulders were shaking with laughter. 'They thought you were a *woo-ya-hoo*. A demon! No wonder they ran.'

'Yeah.' A grin tilted across his mouth. 'well, whatever they thought, it worked. I waited a couple of hours, but there wasn't a sign of them.' He took her hand and brought it to his chest. 'I figured it was safe to go back to you, that there was no risk they'd sneak back and follow me...' He drew a deep breath. 'But when I got to the shack, you were gone.'

Brionny nodded. 'Yes. Father Ramón—'

'Had found you. Yes, I know that now. But then—then, I couldn't imagine what had happened. Had you stumbled into the river and become dinner for another snake? Had the Mali-Mali doubled back and taken you?' His arms swept around her and he held her to him with fierce determination. 'I searched for two days, praying to find you—and afraid of what I'd find if I did.'

'Slade—I didn't know—'

'Eventually, I stumbled into Father Ramón's village. He told me he'd sent you upriver with his men. I went after you—but I was too late. You'd left for the States.' His smile was swift and hard. 'And the police decided to put me up in jail as their guest.'

'Oh, God,' Brionny whispered. 'I'm so sorry! I didn't know—'

'It was an interesting couple of days, Stuart, I'll say that.

Impulsively, she reached up and kissed his mouth. 'I love you,' she said fiercely. 'I'd never want anything bad to happen to you...'

Her hand flew to her mouth, but it was too late. The words she hadn't even permitted herself to think were in the open.

Slade smiled. 'Do you, now?' he said, very softly.

Brionny's cheeks flamed. 'Finish your story,' she said, her chin uplifted. 'How did you get out of jail?'

'It wasn't easy. It took me two days just to get word to my office in Rio to tell them to fly somebody down and sort things out.'

'Your—your office in Rio?'

He nodded. 'Later, one of my vice-presidents pointed

out that I'd have been better off calling my New York office, or the one in Miami— Bree? What is it?'

She had gone white as a sheet. 'What—what are you talking about, McClintoch? What offices in New York and—and Miami—and—and—?'

'Rio,' he said helpfully. 'Well, of course we have offices in Houston and LA too, but—'

Brionny closed her eyes, then opened them again.

'I take it you're—you're not talking about opening offices to—to supervise the theft of—of antiquities,' she said in a faint voice.

Slade chuckled. 'No, sweetheart, I'm not. I suppose I should have told you sooner—hell, I tried to tell you sooner… I'm President, CEO, and the guy generally in charge of Worldwide Construction.'

'Worldwide Con… The company building that road in Peru?'

'Yeah,' he said with a modest smile, 'that's the one.'

Brionny slammed her fists against his shoulders. 'You bastard! You let me think—'

'I let you think what you wanted to think,' he said, catching hold of her wrists. 'You took one look at me and saw a bum.'

'I—I—' She stared at him, and suddenly she knew the truth. 'I—I saw a ghost,' she whispered. 'Someone hurt me, a long time ago, and—and I thought I saw him again when I saw you. It was wrong, I know that now, but—'

'Yeah.' He blew out his breath. 'I guess I looked at you and saw a ghost, too, a specter from my childhood, when I was always the kid who had to prove himself over and over…'

Brionny reached up and kissed him again. It was a

longer kiss this time, and when it ended they were both smiling.

'Slade?' Brionny moved closer into his arms. 'Were you really going to—to demand payment from me last night?'

He brushed a soft kiss over her mouth. 'That was the plan. At least, I told myself it was. I think I really had some crazy idea that if I got you in my arms again I could make you admit you loved me as much as I loved you, but—'

'Do you?' she whispered. 'Love me, I mean?'

'Yes,' he said, 'with all my heart.'

'You'd better mean it. Because if you don't—if you don't, I'll—I'll—'

Laughing, Slade scooped her into his arms. 'What will you do? Whip out your gun and shoot me?' He kissed her, then let her down slowly to her feet. 'Darling Bree. Will you marry me?'

Would she marry him, her handsome renegade? Of course she would. He might not have stolen the emerald, but he had surely stolen her heart.

'I should tell you that you weren't entirely wrong about me,' he said. 'I've spent most of my life bouncing from one construction site to another—but if you marry me I promise to settle down.'

Brionny kissed him. 'You don't have to,' she sighed. 'To tell you the truth, McClintoch, I think I'd like to try my hand at being a bum for a while.'

His arms tightened around her. 'I'm supposed to be in Bora-Bora next week. How does that sound for a honeymoon, Stuart?'

'It sounds wonderful.'

He kissed her again, and when the kiss grew deep

and heated he drew back and gave her an unsteady
smile.

'I think we should carry on this conversation in a
more private setting. I happen to know this apartment
on the East Side with a great view of the river.'

Brionny laughed softly. 'I love places with views of
the river.'

And, with that, Slade swept Brionny into his arms
and carried her out of the director's office, through the
Great Hall, and down the wide marble steps of the museum to the street.

HARLEQUIN ◆ PRESENTS®

The world's bestselling romance series...
The series that brings you your favorite authors,
month after month:

Helen Bianchin...Emma Darcy
Lynne Graham...Penny Jordan
Miranda Lee...Sandra Morton
Anne Mather...Carole Mortimer
Susan Napier...Michelle Reid

and many more uniquely talented authors!

Wealthy, powerful, gorgeous men...
Women who have feelings just like your own...
The stories you love, set in exotic, glamorous locations...

HARLEQUIN PRESENTS,
Seduction and passion guaranteed!

Visit us at www.romance.net

Back by popular demand are

DEBBIE MACOMBER's

Hard Luck, Alaska, is a
town that needs women!
And the O'Halloran brothers
are just the fellows
to fly them in.

Starting in March 2000 this beloved series returns
in special 2-in-1 collector's editions:

MAIL-ORDER MARRIAGES, featuring
Brides for Brothers and *The Marriage Risk*
On sale March 2000

FAMILY MEN, featuring
Daddy's Little Helper and *Because of the Baby*
On sale July 2000

THE LAST TWO BACHELORS, featuring
Falling for Him and *Ending in Marriage*
On sale August 2000

Collect and enjoy each MIDNIGHT SONS story!

Available at your favorite retail outlet.

HARLEQUIN®
Makes any time special ™

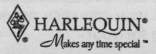